THE VIRGIN NEXT DOOR

LAUREN BLAKELY

ABOUT

Raise your hand if you've ever done this. Written a racy message and sent it to—*oops*—the wrong person.

Yeah, me too. Except, I sent my latest *Tales of a Naughty Virgin* column detailing my fantasies about my hot, charming, thoroughly bangable next-door-neighbor to…MY ENTIRE COMPANY.

Did I mention I'm a children's book editor?

Well, I *was*.

Facepalm

At least the column goes viral, but I'm still the gal who gets fired for her not-safe-for-work thoughts about the so-called "Mister Sexy Pants."

Now I need a job stat, so I jump on the first opportunity. And I come face to face with my new boss.

Mister Sexy Pants himself.

Item number one on my to-do list? Make sure my boss never finds out his alter ego…since all of New York knows I want Mister Sexy Pants to punch my virgin club card.

A DATING GAMES NOVEL

By Lauren Blakely

To be the first to find out when all of my upcoming books go live click here!

PRO TIP: Add lauren@laurenblakely.com to your contacts before signing up to make sure the emails go to your inbox!

Did you know this book is also available in audio and paperback on all major retailers? Go to my website for links!

MISTER SEXY PANTS

THE VIRGIN NEXT DOOR begins with a prequel story, **MISTER SEXY PANTS**. If you already read this prequel when it was released on its own, go ahead and start at **THE VIRGIN NEXT DOOR** ! If not, then start right here and turn the page.

Xoxo

Lauren

ABOUT

Note to self: When meeting a hot, flirty guy be sure to, ya know, get his name.

It might be helpful if you want to see the guy again.

Or, maybe try writing an anonymous s-e-x column about him and see if that gets his attention, starting it like this...

Hello, Mister Sexy Pants. Let me tell you about my fantasies.

1

ALL THE LITTLE SEX MONKEYS

Veronica

Have you ever wanted something so badly that it takes you completely by surprise?

Your desire starts like a low hum, turns into a sweet tingle, then . . . *blastoff*. It rockets into an intense, naked longing.

I've gotten that feeling with books, with dogs, and definitely with sandwiches. But I didn't expect to feel this way about five hundred weekly words, but now that the opportunity to write a dating column dangles in front of me, I've got to grab this carrot no matter what.

That's where my head is at now as I prep for a secret side hustle meeting. I want to nail every aspect of this *job* interview, right down to the look.

I zip up my dress. Smoothing a hand along my waist, I consider my reflection in the mirror on the closet door in my bedroom.

My cat eyes me with imperious suspicion from one of the pillows on my bed.

I think I look smashing, but a woman cannot dress on her opinion alone. That's why my sister is here. I spin around, skirt twirling, and put the question to Hazel, who is sitting on the edge of the bed with my tiny dog curled up in her lap.

"What do you think? Is this what you'd wear to an interview to become a sex columnist?"

I could ask Google, but I'm scared to hear the Internet's thoughts on this fashion quandary.

Hazel screws up the corner of her lips giving me a long once-over, then renders her ruling: "You look like you have a secret."

I smile coyly. "So it's perfect, then, for an anonymous column," I say with a little jut of the hip.

"Come to think of it, yes," she says with a smile.

"Hey! That's a good one." I scurry out to the kitchen, grab a notebook from the table, and jot "Come to think of it" on a list of Top Five Awesome Column Titles.

I snap the notebook closed, then snag my purse. Before I take off, I kiss my pets goodbye, and I head out, Hazel following me.

When we reach the sidewalk, my sister gives me a hug. "You'll be great. There's no one more qualified for this gig than you."

"Maybe this is why I've been waiting for twenty-six years. I've been holding out for an online column," I say playfully.

"I mean, it's not a bad reason to wait," she says drily as we let go.

Then we say goodbye, and I turn toward Hudson Street. As the spring sun dips in the sky, I review my original pitch for the online site The Dating Pool—*what about a sex and dating column written from the point of view of a virgin?*

The column only requires a few hours a week, and though I definitely don't want to leave my job as a children's book editor, I do love talking about sex, writing about sex, and thinking about it.

I'm sure I'd like sex, if I ever had it.

But if I can nab this project, I'll have an outlet at last for all the little sex monkeys rattling their cages in my head.

Watch out, Dating Pool. Here comes one opinionated, battery-operated-boyfriend-loving virgin who believes a dirty mind's a terrible thing to waste.

* * *

When I reach The Dating Pool's office, I stop and stare up at the building, taking in the sleek facade. In a moment ripped from a rom-com, I'm *that woman* stepping into the big, wide world of New York media. Only, I've grown up in and around this city. I love New York, and New York loves me.

Chin up, lipstick on, I head inside. The elevator shoots me up to the fifth floor, where the helpful receptionist escorts me to Bellamy Hart's office.

She's a romance goddess, and her podcast is an absolute must-listen. She's also a total badass boss babe and she looks the part in her designer jeans, spiky boots, and black twinset.

"Thank you for coming in at the last minute," she says as she holds the door open to her office.

"Thank you for asking me here," I say, already a little giddy. She replied to my email ten minutes after I sent it last night. I might very well frame her note. *I must hear more! Do not take your idea elsewhere.*

Well then, here I am.

We sit on her green couch, and she waggles her tablet. "First of all, let me say your column ideas completely grabbed me. I agree that columns of dating lists, dating dos and don'ts, and dating rules are so overdone," she says with a sigh. "But your takes sound fresh."

I sit straighter and fight off a smile—I won't crack open the champagne yet. "It's a good thing I've been storing them up from a few years on the New York dating market, aka the alligator pit. And I can tackle them in a way that appeals to all your readers—with a little humor," I say.

I elaborate on my ideas: Ten Things People Assume About Virgins, Sex Tips from Those Who Haven't, How to Break the News to Your Date, Wear Whatever You Want, and Other Things You Could Be Doing Tonight. "I see it as the dating misadventures of a virgin with a naughty mind."

Bellamy sighs deeply, then smiles. "I can see the clicks going up, up, up. When can you start?"

My heart bounces. "I can send you my first column this week."

I, Veronica Valentine, children's book editor by day, am about to become an anonymous sexpert by night.

2

MAN DESSERT

Veronica

This kind of opportunity calls for a celebration.

Since my sister's on deadline with her next novel, I text my friend Ellie and ask if she has time to meet me for a slice of cake.

Ellie: We have an evening shoot, and I'm due on set in forty-five minutes, but I can meet you for ten of them, and I promise to make it the best ten minutes of your day.

Veronica: I don't know about that, honey. The ten minutes I spent with The Flyer this morning were pretty damn good. But time with you is always a treat too.

Ellie: As if I'd try to compete with The Flyer. No mere mortal, man or woman, ever could.

Veronica: I suspect that's entirely true. See you at Peace of Cake.

I walk to my favorite cake shop in the city, stopping at the gleaming white storefront in Chelsea. A selection of mouth-watering delights beckons me from the lavish window display—luscious chocolate slices, delicate pink frosting on sponge cake, festive mint green slathered over vanilla.

This is heaven.

I push open the door, hunting for my friend in the empty shop, which closes in thirty minutes. I don't see Ellie, but I find an absolutely stunning piece of dessert behind the counter.

Man dessert.

I'm gonna need a minute to gawk.

Hello, hottie. With a trim beard, strong jaw, and inked arms, the man arranging cakes in the display case belongs on the cover of one of my sister's romance novels.

I'll buy a dozen copies, thank you very much.

The man turns my way and flashes me a smile that zings straight down my body. Make that two-dozen copies.

I smile back, and as I head to the counter, my phone pings with a new text from my friend.

Ellie: Running late. Please forgive me. If you must start without me, I understand. Cake is just too hard to resist.

But cake isn't the thing I'm going to have a hard time resisting.

Staring is.

At the counter, I meet the gaze of the blue-eyed man with a winning smile. "What can I do for you?" he asks. "We've got cake if that's what you're in the market for. But if you're looking for the meaning of the universe, I make no promises."

That's a hell of an opening line, and it makes me laugh. It also challenges me to come up with something that matches the promise of him. "Are you fending off that many requests for existential answers?"

"I am. But the slogan says it all." He points to the words on his apron. *Cake Is Proof.*

"That makes perfect sense." I meet his playful gaze with one of my own. "Cake is, indeed, proof there is meaning in my universe."

"What a wonderful universe," he says with a spark that makes me want to keep playing word ping-pong.

"But I might have to add dogs and books to the evidence," I say. "I hope you don't mind the addendum."

He scoffs. "Do I look like the type of person who's bothered by addendums?"

I arch a brow, resisting a smile. "What does that type of person look like? I'm trying to draw a mental picture and I'm coming up blank."

"What would they look like?" He points his thumbs at his chest. "Not this guy. I think addendums are fantastic. Especially when they involve books, dogs, *beer*, and cake."

I'm giddy from the flirting. It's almost too good to be true. "But see, I don't think I'd include beer in my favorites. We'll just have to agree on three out of four for our list."

"Fair enough," he says. "I can work with a seventy-five percent match."

Match.

I'm zipping inside. "So, what's good here these days?" I ask, glancing toward the cake selection.

"Is this your first time here?"

"No way. I'm definitely not a Peace of Cake virgin," I say, savoring the way the V-word rolls off my tongue like sugar—and what it does to him.

His eyes darken. His nostrils flare. He takes a beat, then says, "Then you should have a little of everything. It's our special today."

"Tempting. What does a little of everything taste like?" I ask, hoping no one else comes in the shop this evening. An unlikely scenario, since Peace of Cake is almost always deluged with last-minute customers before it closes. This sliver of time with Mister Flirt will end all too soon.

"It tastes like what you should have." The rasp of his voice thrums deliciously across all my erogenous zones, which, right now, include every single molecule in and on me. Then he exhales heavily, as if he's recalibrating. Downshifting. "But I'd also recommend the vanilla celebration cake. It goes with polka dots," he says, his gaze sailing up and down my dress.

"I'll take it."

As he moves to the display case, strong arms reaching in to grab the cake, I try to look away. And I fail miserably. I am officially an ogler.

True, I have a thing for blazing guns like his. But I'm omnivorous, really. I want toned arms, kind eyes, a clever brain, and a big heart.

I want it all. That's probably why I'm holding my V-card at age twenty-six. I haven't met someone who revs my engine on all cylinders.

I'm not sure one guy in a cake shop will tick all my boxes, but I'd like to learn how many checkmarks he can make.

He glances my way. "Want me to bring this to you at a table or the cake bar?"

There is only one answer. The cake bar runs along the counter. If I sit there, I can keep talking with him.

"The cake bar," I say with a small smile as I move away from the register and along the counter, where I pop onto a tall metal stool.

"Good choice," he murmurs. He slides a sharp knife through the cake, then serves it, handing me the plate and a fork. "I hope you enjoy it, Miss Polka Dot."

I roam my gaze over him. "I hope so too, Mister Dessert."

He smiles and then turns away to wash his hands. I check my phone. I'm a terrible friend for hoping Ellie might be later still.

The universe must be granting wishes today because a new message blinks up at me.

Ellie: Don't hate me, but I can't make it. Trains are slow, and I need to get to the set!

Veronica: I'm glad you didn't make it, and I'll tell you why later.

Then I put the phone away and take a bite of cake, chased by flirty, dirty hope.

3

OTHER WORDS FOR DATING

Milo

Dear Self,

Joel did not ask you to fill in today to flirt with his customers. You are here to serve cake while he takes his wife—your very good friend—to an ultrasound appointment. You are not here, you dirty stinking pervert, to check out the absolute fox in the pink dress with the white polka dots, with that chestnut hair curling just so over her shoulders and those plush, red lips. Nope. You are here as a good friend and absolutely nothing more.

Sincerely, the Angel on Your Shoulder

. . .

Except, what's so wrong with flirting? It's not like anything is going to come of it. I know better than to get involved because dating leads to disaster, and I've got the scars to prove it.

But it's been a while since I've had a great conversation, and I doubt I'll see this woman again.

Angel, stand down. Devil, you're up.

I hang around her side of the cake bar as she picks up her fork and takes a bite of the slice in front of her.

"Mmm. Ten out of ten. That's my review."

"Are you a reviewer?" I ask, bracing myself. Online reviews are the bane of my existence.

Laughing, she shakes her head. "Nope. But I could leave one on Google if you'd like."

Aww, that's sweet. "I appreciate it, but there's no need. The Internet is a terrible thing. We should abolish it."

She shoots me a doubtful look. "Damn. We were vibing for a while there, Mister Dessert. We might be three out of five now."

I groan, over the top style, as I wipe down the counter. "Nooo. Don't break my heart. You love the Internet? Imagine how much nicer people would be to each other if they didn't have the keyboard and a screen to hide behind."

To hide their lies.

"I'll grant you that, but I'm not one of those Internet haters. You're not going to be able to back me up against that wall," she says, dipping the fork into the frosting.

I'd like to back her up against the wall, hike up that dress, and grind against her.

She brings the fork to those lush lips, then licks off the frosting, savoring it, doing indecent things to the utensil with her tongue.

I whimper.

Must focus. I shake off the dirty thoughts like a dog getting out of the shower. "You know how it goes. You're in synch. You're out of synch. Before I know it, you're going to tell me you don't like"—I pause to cast about for something universally beloved—"flowers."

She scoffs. "C'mon. That was a softball. Who would possibly hate flowers?"

I laugh, then set down the rag next to the sink. "Sometimes you need softballs. So we are officially back to four out of six. Which is sixty-six percent, if you were wondering." I wiggle a brow like I just said the sexiest thing.

"You are such a percentage showoff."

I take a bow, then park my hands on the counter. "What they don't tell you in middle school is that percentages are the only math you'll ever really need as an adult."

"I call them the unsung heroes of math," she says, then waggles the fork my way. "Want a bite?"

I want to bite her shoulder. Lick her neck. Nibble on her earlobe. "I would, but I can't eat on the job," I whisper, shaking my head in faux annoyance. "The boss is such a hard ass."

"Oh, I bet he is," she says.

"He's the worst," I tease, because Joel runs a tight ship. "So I must resist your very tempting offer."

"Your loss," she says, then pops the bite in her mouth and moans around it.

Kill. Me. Now.

I try to focus on something else. Anything. What did we last talk about? Oh, right. Math. "But I admit that arithmetic has its uses."

She brandishes her fork as if to punctuate my point. "I will see your arithmetic and will add fractions."

"Caught you there. Fractions *are* percentages, Miss Polka Dot," I say. "You can't count them twice."

"I know that. Do you have something against synonyms now too? Sheesh. Sometimes we need more than one way of saying something," she says, a little challenging. "I say we keep fractions *and* percentages."

Am I actually getting turned on by her fast brain? Oh hell yes, I am. "I would never, ever want to abolish synonyms," I say.

"I probably wouldn't return here if you did. That'd be the end of this whole thing," she says, waving from me to her.

This thing.

Could this thing lead to one hot night?

Devil says yes.

I should fill in for Iris's hubby more often. "Shame. I wouldn't want that to happen. So, on our favorites list, we'll keep synonyms, percentages, and how about . . ." My gaze drifts toward the window as the sun shines, unseasonably warm, on an April afternoon. "We add sunny days in April."

She hums her approval. "It sounds like we have an agreement, then."

"I believe we do, Miss Polka Dot," I say, and I'm this close to asking her out for coffee.

Coffee's just coffee, after all. It won't even count as breaking my no-dating-this-year vow. And coffee could lead to one hot night between the sheets.

But before I can ask, the door swings open, and a gaggle of teenage girls pours in. So much for synonyms for dating.

4

———

NAME THAT CRUSH

Veronica

He's busy.

No big deal. He runs the place, I bet, so I'll come back another time.

I don't want to be pushy. I do want to give him time to do his job. But when I finish my treat, the place is still a zoo.

I bus my own plate, setting it in the wash bin under the utensil counter, then I spin back around. The line still snakes around the display case. Another time.

I catch his eye and wave as I mouth, *goodbye.*

He gives a *what-can-you-do* smile, then waves back.

I leave, a little happier and a little sadder.

* * *

A few days later, nerves sweep through my chest as I near Peace of Cake. I can turn around. Abandon this mission. Grab a book, curl up with my pets, watch a show with Ellie.

I don't *need* to see that man again. I don't *need* to get his name. I can just go.

But then I remember the way I felt when he looked into my eyes—*swoopy*.

Nerves be damned. I'm doing this. My flats click-clack across the sidewalk as I near the white shop with its pink and green awning, its sparkling window, its promise of culinary pleasure.

I want other pleasures, and I want to explore them with him.

Deep breath.

I grab the door and head inside.

My shoulders drop, my heart thudding to the ground.

He's not behind the counter. Some other guy is—a teenager with red hair and a freckled face.

I march up to him. "Hi, I'm wondering if that guy with the beard and the blue eyes is here?" I ask, and wow, I sound like a creepy stalker.

His brow knits. "Oh, Joel's friend. Nope. He doesn't work here. He was helping out that day."

I swallow past the weirdness of my next question. "Oh, does he have a name?"

The guy scratches his chin. "Michael? Matthew? Mateo? One of those. If not, it was definitely Robert," he says, then another customer strolls in, and I feel exactly twelve hundred percent sillier than I felt five minutes ago.

Hmm. I guess I do need percentages.

* * *

A couple weeks later, I'm pacing across my balcony, trying to figure out what I want to write about for my third column. The first two ticked their way to the top of The Dating Pool's most popular article list, so I need to keep the streak alive.

I walk along my tiny patio, back and forth past the little ceramic pots in my city garden, mulling over ideas.

I need a killer starting line, but I don't quite have it yet so I step inside, grab my metal watering can and fill it up at the sink. Then I return to my deck, watering the little pots of sage that I recently planted, then the kale, the pole beans and the rosemary too.

I set down the can as my cat, Hot Stuff, rubs against my ankle, purring as he marks me. Bending down, I stroke his soft head for a bit, then stand and lean against the brick railing, checking out my patch of Grove Street, lined with pretty trees stretching their branches in the spring. It's the kind of block where you might shoot a movie. The kind of block where anything feels possible.

Resting my elbows on the edge of the brick, I watch the evening roll by.

My heart thumps a little faster as the silhouette of a man comes into view below. Closer, then even closer. I recognize those strong arms, that square jaw, the delicious amount of scruff.

That's him. "Mister Dessert," I call out.

But he keeps walking because . . . earbuds.

Damn earbuds.

He's probably listening to a baking podcast about making delicious cake for the woman you can't stop thinking about. I try to wave too, but he doesn't look up.

Le sigh.

Then he passes me, and I get a back view for the first time.

Oh. My. Stars.

Did I just become an ass woman?

I think so.

I can't look away from his booty. My eyes are drawn to his perfect tush, and his fantastic pants—trim, checked, blue. They're fashionable and such a welcome change from what most men wear—baggy, boring cargo shorts or too-loose jeans or, barf, khakis. "I shall call him Mister Sexy Pants," I declare, as he turns into a nearby building.

I don't feel so silly anymore. I feel . . . inspired. I break out my phone and dictate my column.

5

HIS FIRST APPEARANCE

Veronica

The Virgin Club
Breaking the Good News to Your Date

If you're going to have a crush, you might as well name that crush. I gave mine a name today.

I call him Mister Sexy Pants. I've seen him around once or twice. Fine, fine, one time we talked, the other time I just stared like a peeping Tom as he walked past me on the street below.

But I don't think anyone could blame me. He's witty, funny, and so easy on the eyes.

He's also become the object of my fantasies. Yep. I'm not afraid to admit I've whispered my crush's name alone at night with my battery-operated friends.

I've asked him to do unholy things to my body alone in the dark.

Hell, I've begged.

Which makes me wonder . . .

How would I tell him about my V-card if we ever had the chance?

The *reveal* is a thing the unplucked have to consider.

Some might think a virgin's top worry is how it'll feel when she finally does the deed. And, if you're into guys, there's the will-it-fit question.

Me? The thing that keeps me up at night is how I'm going to break the ice.

If we go out for drinks, do I order a virgin Piña Colada, give the drink a coquettish look, then say, *The cocktail isn't the only virgin here?*

Or I could say, *Wanna put your Piña in my Colada sometime?*

Maybe I take him shopping for olive oil, hold up a bottle of extra virgin and say, *This, me, same.*

But those feel twee.

Then there's the super direct approach. Over a cup of coffee, I could clear my throat, then say, "Hey, I haven't ever tried reverse cowgirl, girl on top, doggy style, or any variation on the above, but I'd really like to with you."

First date, fifth date, text, in person? What's a never-been-touched-down-there gal to do? Do you treat it like a secret or a fact?

I'm here to tell you the choice is all yours. There is no right or wrong way. You don't owe it to anyone to reveal it in *their* time. Do it in your own time.

Say it when you meet. Or don't say it when you meet. Share it over drinks or coffee. Or don't. Wait till the fifth date or the tenth or the first. It's your virginity. It's not anyone else's.

As for me, when I meet the right guy, I'll probably keep it simple and say something like, "Want to go where only a battery-operated friend has gone before?"

Until then, I'll be picturing Mister Sexy Pants . . .

Your Friendly Neighborhood Virgin

6

———

THE SYNONYM SLINGER

Milo

A month or so later . . .

Today is the day.

I am wound like a top.

All my bones are cranked tight, my nerves stretched thin.

I've been waiting for this chance for months. But before I walk into this hornet's nest of a meeting, I need to burn off my worries, so I cruise along the High Line on my bike.

My thighs throbbing and my lungs burning, I rehearse the lines I practiced with my brother so I won't flub them in front of the lawyers. As I fly, the warm June wind whipping past me, I prep in my head till the words are second nature.

I run down my mental checklist again as I exit the High Line and cut across town to my block. I have all the documentation. I have all the information I need to make my point.

I turn onto my street, head down, when, whoa . . .

There she is.

The cake babe. The witty woman. The clever, fork-licking, synonym slinger. I haven't seen her since that day in the cake shop.

And I'm seeing her now, on my block, the very second I have someplace else to be?

Are you fucking kidding me, universe?

And even though I'm still running far away from dating and the disasters it brings, I've been secretly hoping I'd bump into her again. Hell, I've been wishing she'd appear.

Ever since the day I met her, I've imagined this scenario.

So today, of all days, the universe delivers the fork-licker?

Thanks a fucking lot, Fate.

Now is the worst possible moment. I can't afford any distraction...

Find out about Milo's plans and Veronica's plans and how Murphy's Law is about to capsize all of them in THE VIRGIN NEXT DOOR ...

THE *virgin* NEXT DOOR
#1 New York Times Bestselling Author
LAUREN BLAKELY

THE VIRGIN NEXT DOOR

HER PROLOGUE

I Shall Call Him Mister Sexy Pants

I know a thing or two about fetishes thanks to my super-secret dating-in-the-city column, but I didn't know about my own fetish until it began a few months ago. I'd just landed the column gig, so I took myself out to celebrate, as one does, with cake.

The guy who served me the slice at Peace of Cake was sexy and clever, and we flirted over frosting for a few minutes, talking about nerdy things like fractions and synonyms. But then, a pack of teenagers swarmed the shop. I had to go, and I never got his name. He called me Miss Polka Dot. I called him Mister Dessert.

I returned a few days later, but he wasn't there. Turned out he'd just been helping out a friend. I had no idea where to find him.

C'est la vie.

But a month after that, I was sitting on my third-floor balcony of my apartment in the Village, watching New York go by in the spring, when I spotted him walking down the street. And what a view. This specimen of bearded, inked modern man wasn't picking his clothes from the conventional dude-drobe of baggy pants, loose jeans, or Boring-with-a-capital-B khakis. He was clearly dressing for my delight in those trim, checked pants that hugged his legs.

Thank you, Mister Sexy Pants.

I, Veronica Valentine, had discovered a brand-new kink. I had a thing for men wearing trendy, tight trousers, as I went on to detail the following week in my anonymous column, *The Virgin Club.*

But then, a little while after that, life happened, things happened, trouble happened, and my crush crashed into the middle of my life, where I'd have to see him every single stinking day.

The plan? Make sure he never, ever knows he's the one and only Mister Sexy Pants.

1

MY GLITTER DEALER

Veronica

A tiny speck of glitter floats through the afternoon light from the living room window, like dandelion fluff. Then, it hovers above my keyboard and parachutes onto the letter Q.

Oh, hell no.

Glitter is the devil.

I flick at it, but the obstinate turkey won't vacate the key. I lean forward in my vinyl kitchen chair, then blow on the enemy.

Bye, bye, you glittery imp. You will not ruin my editorial letter to Agnes Millicent.

With the keyboard again pristine, I return to my letter to one of the cleverest children's book writers of this generation. I'm ready to tell her how she can tease out the conflict between the frog and the prince a smidge more when . . . bastard!

Another emerald particle skydives onto the keyboard.

I head to the bathroom, my tan Chihuahua trotting gamely behind me because no woman is allowed to use the restroom without her dog. I check out my reflection, and what the hell? My neck shimmers like tinsel on a Christmas tree.

"Did you knock a tube of glitter onto me, StudMuffin?" I ask my boy.

Big bat ears pop up like radar dishes, but he doesn't confess. He tilts his head in the direction of . . . of course.

The sleeping Siamese lies posed like an odalisque, his rotund body stretched across the hall floor.

"I mean, maybe he did it," I say to the dog. "Cats are like butlers."

This glitter could be left over from the Little Artists class I taught yesterday at the creativity co-op over on Christopher Street. Grabbing a washcloth from the shelf behind me in the bathroom, I daub at the emerald sparkles on my throat, trying valiantly to Sherlock Holmes my way through the Case of the Glittery Neck.

Hmm.

That new silk scarf my sister lent me—well, I lifted it from her wardrobe last weekend, but those are sister's rights—did have a little sheen to it. I scrub my skin clean, then return to the kitchen table, ready to conquer this letter, one that will surely impress my editorial director, who'll then promote me, lauding me as one of the most talented editors ever at McGee Whitney Books for Young Readers.

StudMuffin whines at my feet as soon as I start typing. I invite him into my lap, patting my bare legs. Pants can suck it on remote-work days.

He doesn't jump but instead races to the door in a flurry of tan fur and desperation. "Hold on, handsome. I'll be right there."

I dart to my bedroom and grab the red polka-dot skirt I left on the bureau after art class and pull it on. One pocket sags, and I stuff my hand in, groping around. Ah, there's a tube of glitter from class yesterday, a lipstick, and I think my pair of skull earrings with the missing hook. But I have to jet, so I leave the treasure trove intact. Then I snag the scarf, because I am not going to offend Manhattan by showing them my nest of unwashed hair.

No way.

I fly to the door, leash up my pooch, and stuff my feet in flats. We rocket down the three flights in my walkup building, sprint out to Grove Street, and arrive at his favorite tree just in time for the little guy to make his mark in Manhattan.

I catch my breath as he whizzes.

Man. Nothing like the fear of dog pee to make a gal run. As StudMuffin does his business, I scan the busy block for . . . well, for anything out of place. New York seems to be under construction these days, so my street has become a postcard for scaffolding. A cement truck swings onto my block, and then I hear a whisking noise.

Dammit. I know that sound. I *have* to know that sound.

I spot the cyclist as he hops from the street onto the

sidewalk to avoid the truck. This is bad. The guy on the bike is now twenty feet away, and my dog hates bikes as much as I hate bad grammar. "StudMuffin!" I warn as he lowers his leg at last.

My brown-eyed boy glances innocently at me while I tug on his leash. I'm about to scoop him up and out of the line of fire when he catches a glimpse of the wheeled velociraptor.

He loses his canine mind. We're talking ear-splitting howls of bike rage as he prepares to ambush the two-wheeler, now five feet away.

I lunge for StudMuffin before he can attack the front wheel. Immediately, the cyclist yanks the handlebars and steers the bike into the tree, stumbling off it, but landing on his feet. "Whoa," he mutters as I hug the dog to my chest, my pulse spiking.

I whip around to face the cyclist.

It's . . . holy hell . . . no way.

My dog bike-tripped Mister Sexy Pants. The hot, clever guy I talked to once upon a time in a cake shop a few months ago. The guy whose name I never got.

His back is to me as he untangles his . . . pants leg.

Gah. Not helpful. His butt is so cute in those tight pants.

Think fast, Veronica.

I huff out a breath. Check. Cinnamon-y.

I lift a hand to my wild hair. Thank goddess I hid it in a scarf.

A breeze blows by. It's summer, so the air feels good on my legs.

The guy straightens and peers at me, studying my face, then my body.

"Oh. Hi. Miss Polka Dot," he says, using the nickname he gave me that day at the shop. He remembers, which is awesome, but a little terrifying, considering my state of attire. "Um. You . . . well, you have . . ." he says in a voice straight out of my daydreams. And my night dreams. And my dirty dreams.

I flash a self-deprecating smile as I lift a hand absently to my neck. "My neck is covered in glitter. I thought I got it all off, but I must have missed some," I say.

But he doesn't laugh. He winces like he's borderline embarrassed.

"Actually," he begins, swallowing, then stopping. He was smooth the day I chatted with him in the cake shop, but he's awkward now and it's so cute. I love awkward men. They're such a breath of fresh air. "It's not your neck. It's your . . ."

He points, lowering his hand in the general direction of my . . . fresh air.

My ass!

That's why there's a breeze.

I slap my hand to my butt, and it's swinging in the summer breeze. I hurriedly tug my obstinate skirt hem out of the waistband of my panties.

Where it's been the whole time.

Great. Just great. I've been flashing New York City my cheeky black panties with pink cartoon devils on them since I hightailed it out of my home.

My *other* cheeks heat, my face surely the shade of a candy apple. Setting my dog down, I swing around, smoothing my skirt one more time when StudMuffin barks, lunging at the bike. I spin back to grab him but as I whirl, the contents of my pockets clatter to the sidewalk.

Ugh.

This is not my day.

Squatting, I reach for the lipstick, its brand name like an advertisement for all my naughty fantasies—*Come to Bed Red*. Yup, I'm a beet now. Holding the bike, he bends to grab the glitter tube.

My swoon meter shoots sky-high. Mister Sexy Pants is a gallant gentleman.

Come to bed, indeed. Maybe he'll ask for my number next, offer to make me a panini, then indulge my balcony fantasies.

"Here you go," he says, holding out the glitter, his fingers grazing against mine, and oh my god, the invite is coming in three, two, one . . .

Then the top pops off the tube and a spray of green glitter spews up onto his sexy, whiskery beard. He's sooo going to rescind the panini and post-panini offer before he even makes it.

"I'm sorry. The tops are kind of . . . kludgy," I say, as I roam my gaze over his emerald-green beard. He looks like a leprechaun, and why in the holy hell is he still sexy?

Hot guys can get away with anything, but I feel awful. This is all my fault. *Obviously.* "I'm sorry for the glitter bomb," I say. This was not how I was supposed to encounter Mister Sexy Pants from the cake shop convo.

He was supposed to stride up to me some evening when I looked stunning and smart coming from the office, being all sexy librarian and sandwich-worthy, not like a hot mess express in cheek-revealing panties.

Wincing, I brace myself for him to go all growly dickhead on me and grumble out a "Watch what you're doing, miss."

But he flicks some specks off his scruff, then retrieves the top from the ground and hands it to me. "Glitter tops are the worst. Next time, I'll be sure to give you the number of my glitter dealer," he says all deadpan and charming, and adding kerosene to my crush.

I take the top, a little dazed as he mounts his wheeled steed then adjusts his helmet. Dipping his head maybe, just maybe, to hide a smile, he mutters *pink devils* while he rides away.

As I fasten the top back on the glitter, I am officially both mortified and turned on. Which sums up my life in a nutshell.

2

———

HER DEVIL BUTT

Milo

I'm sure there's a video on YouTube showing how to de-glitter a beard in less than ten seconds.

But right now I'm concentrating on making it to the offices of Moneygrubber & Mercenary on my bike in one piece.

I need to dodge a parked taxi hellbent on door-prizing me. But the cool robotic voice of my LiDAR app warns me that now would be a good time to die if I speed up just as a bus rumbles in the lane next to me. I slow my pace, and once the bus passes, I whoosh by the taxi, my peripheral vision catching a glimpse of the driver idling and smoking a cigarette.

People are the worst.

But do I flip him off? No. Because I am a good guy, contrary to what my ex's menagerie of exes would have the world believe.

I keep pace with traffic on Seventh Avenue for a few blocks until I reach my destination. I slow, then jump to the sidewalk and hop off my bike.

With a wary gulp, I stare up at the ominous black building straight out of a comic book. Cue the *Meanwhile, inside the villain's lair* caption. So fitting. I groan, then groan again. And maybe one more time.

Best to get all my annoyed groans out of my system before I head into arbitration with Miss Lie Her Pants Off Callie.

I bet Miss Cute Devil Butt is nothing like my ex. Hell, she was a delight to chat with that day at the cake shop when I subbed for my buddy. And she upped the ante today, calling me Stud Muffin, after all. Gotta give her points for directness, and that's the total opposite of Callie. Plus, the Glitter Bomber likes dogs for real and looked hella hot clutching her little Chihuahua, so I'll award her a few more points.

Also, she had an absolutely fantastic ass. I tried not to stare too hard today, but I'm no superhero. I'm a mere mortal man who likes a cute, round rear. But let's give it up for her face too, with that spray of freckles across her nose, her clever green eyes, and lips that looked kissable whether she was wearing the *Come to Bed Red* lipstick that fell from her pocket or not.

Whoa.

I pump the brakes on the dirty-mind train.

I can't think flirty, dirty thoughts about a woman, no matter how much I'd been hoping to bump into her again.

I have a mission.

This second, I'm Milo the Impervious, and I must vanquish the enemy and retrieve the treasure.

After I unclip my helmet, I carry my bike into the lobby, quickly scanning the list of businesses on the wall. The arbitrators are on the fifth floor, so I head to the freight elevator and punch the button.

As the lift shoots up, I square my shoulders, determined to keep my wits about me for the next few hours. I've got to get my dog back.

I must be strong and fearless. And I can't go into the meeting looking like the Jolly Green Giant jizzed on my beard.

Taking out my phone, I click on the search bar, then speak: "Google, how do you remove glitter from a beard?"

"To remove glitter from a beard, Reddit recommends *shave it off, you dumbass.*"

I roll my eyes. "Fuck you, Google," I mutter as the elevator arrives and the doors slide open. I'll just wash my beard. Take that, search engine. This guy has common sense.

Well, sometimes.

When I step out of the elevator, I forget about glitter beards because the best girl in the whole world lunges at me. My heart bursts with happiness as Trudy tackles me. With one hand on my bike, I kneel to let my dog lick my face. Hell, maybe she can Roomba off the emerald specks.

"I missed you too, little lady," I tell her, and for a few seconds, everything feels right in the world again.

It's been nine long months of only weekend custody

with my girl, but this purgatory will end today. I'm getting my pooch back, no matter what it takes with the arbitrators Callie's lawyers picked.

When I stand, my Min-Pin mix thumping her tail and whining happily, I spot my ex a few feet away. I knew she'd be here. She brought the dog, of course. But I was enjoying that reunion without thinking about her. Now, she's batting her lashes my way, and I have no choice but to deal with Callie.

"Milo, sweetheart. You have glitter in your beard. Let me help you," she says.

Barf.

Like I don't know her shtick—be as sweet as a sugar cookie so no one knows she's draining her beaus of dough while dating other dudes. But I discovered her scheme when boyfriend Number Two contacted me to find out why the hell she was Venmoing *me* money. Um, for the rent. She lived with me while juggling boyfriends Number Three and Number Four too.

Yeah, that was fun.

"It's fine," I say gruffly.

She tuts. "You can't go into arbitration looking like a mess. Let's just make it easy. We can get back together and we'll both get to have Baby."

I refrain from rolling my eyes all the way to the back of my head. Like I'd name a dog *Baby*.

"Thanks, but I'd rather take the subway to work," I say drily, then scan the hall for the bathroom, and, I hope, a bike storage closet.

I pat my thigh. Wiggling her butt, Trudy follows me

as I wheel my bike a few feet away, rehearsing my plan for winning one hundred percent custody.

I've got pictures of the 5Ks Trudy and I ran together in the park, vaccination records going back four years, and even her dog helmet right here with me on my bike, which has a custom-built dog seat for a twenty-pound pup. Plus, I can prove I adopted her from the Little Friends shelter well before I met Callie, and I've got statements from the vet that I've brought her to all her appointments.

The best proof of all? Her loyalty. She's following *me.* I am ready to nail this arbitration.

"Hold on, sweetheart. Let me show you something," Callie coos at my back, then I spin around, and the blonde trickster blows a kiss to the dog. "Gimme a kiss, Baby."

"Her name's not Baby," I spit out.

But my girl wags her tail, rushes to Callie, and lifts her snout to give a kiss. Oh, man. "Trudy, you're killing me," I mutter.

"Stand on your hind legs, Baby" Callie says, and the pooch I took to work every single day complies.

Perfectly.

It wasn't enough for my ex to trick me and three other dudes? She had to hoodwink my dog too?

"Baby also smiles when I say the arbitrator's name. Dennis is a dog lover," she tells me, oh-so sweetly. Then to Trudy, she chirps, "Baby, be a good girl and smile when I say hi to Dennis."

My girl smiles in practice, and I wither.

But I won't let Callie win. My ex-girlfriend stole

from me, stole from the other guys she dated, then told them I was the scammer. Then those guys left shitty reviews for my business online.

Now, she wants to steal my dog *and* give her a cringeworthy name? "What do you want?" I bite out.

Callie flashes me a polished pink grin. "I want you back. I could make you happy, Milo."

"No," I say crisply.

She shrugs, taps her manicured finger against her lip, then stares at the ceiling. After she lets out a big breath, she says, "Then how about five thousand dollars and I'll sign over full custody?"

Does she really think she can manipulate me like this? Wait, stupid question. Of course she does.

I seethe, then gulp at the manipulation. I take one look at my little dog, then whisper, "Trudy, c'mere."

She trots over to me, wiggles her bottom, and licks my face.

"Done."

This is real love. No tricks or treats here.

Love you can trust is priceless.

An hour later, I write a check and leave with my dog. "Romance is bullshit, right, little lady? This is true love right here."

Her tongue wags as I snap on her helmet then secure her in the dog seat on the front of the bike.

She's back where she belongs.

I ride home slowly, taking side streets, careful with

my precious cargo. When I turn onto Grove Street, a flash of silver on the sidewalk catches my attention. Stopping, I dismount the bike and hold the handle while I check out the bounty.

Huh.

A pair of silver skull earrings gleam on the sidewalk.

They have to be Glitter Gal's. I wish I knew her name. It's not like Glitter Gal is a step up from Miss Polka Dot, but it fits the bill. And fits the woman—a woman who wears cartoon pink devil panties would absolutely have silver skull earrings with rhinestones for eyes. Except, one of them is missing a hook.

I pick them up and show them to my pooch. "What do you think, Tru? Should we try to return these? She probably lives on this block. I could even leave my number."

From her seat, my dog tilts her head, like she's frowning in disapproval. Even my dog knows I need to stay far, far away from the suggestion of a date.

"You're right, little lady. No numbers." I'll just try to figure out which building is hers and maybe leave them in an envelope by the door. That'll be all.

I tuck the earrings into my pocket and wheel my bike to my building. When I reach the stoop and undo my dog's seatbelt, I spot the silhouette of a woman on the balcony of the building next door.

It's a brunette with chestnut waves in her hair. Is that her? Glitter Gal?

She bops her head as if listening to music, then swirls and I glimpse her profile, then she shimmies her butt.

I grin wickedly. Yup. I'd recognize that ass anywhere.

"Hey!" I call out. But she doesn't hear since she's caught up in her private dance party.

Ah well, it's for the best.

I'm five thousand dollars in the hole thanks to the last time I dated. But at least I know where she lives so I can return her earrings like the good guy I am, not the swindler Callie's exes have made me out to be.

I go inside my building with my dog, reunited at last.

3

———

I WILL NEVER STOP CHECKING MY SKIRTS

Veronica

My mom taught me that when life hands you lemons, make lemonade.

Like, literally.

A glass of lemonade is the first step to solving a problem, she'd say.

Nice idea from Mama Valentine, but I'm too busy hunting for a time machine because that's the only thing that might erase the perma-pink shade of embarrassment tinging my cheeks.

But I have no luck finding a come-and-get-your-free-do-overs-here card when I return to my apartment post-dog walk, during which I replayed the sad French film *The Loss of the Last Shred of My Dignity* the whole time.

I take the next best route to putting the panty-flashing incident behind me. Stick my head in the sand of work for the rest of the day.

With StudMuffin curled up in his cuddle cup bed, I smooth my hand down my skirt—I will never stop double-checking my skirts. I head to the kitchen table and toggle on my laptop. Time to divert my brainpower to this editorial letter. It'll distract me from the meet-the-hottie again mishap loop in my head, and I can stay ahead of schedule at work. The letter is due in two days, but sending it early will impress my boss, Blanche Thatcher. Blanche loves over-deliverers, so perhaps this letter can help secure my promotion. And, let's be honest, beat out the competition, like Darius Daniels with his sharp editorial eye, and Caroline Lopez, with her firm but loving style.

Opening Microsoft Word, I review what I already wrote pre-ignominious incident. I consult the piece of paper by my laptop—I draft all my editorial letters by hand—then I tweak some of the initial text and finish off the last few lines.

*The tension between archenemies Frog and Prince is exquisite, and the final battle scene on the rickety bridge over the roaring waters sent shivers down my spine as the antagonists parried. Could you tease out that moment even more on those pages? Just add a touch more oomph to the fight, and it'll be *chef's kiss.**

I can't wait to see what you do with this amazing adventure tale!

· · ·

Sincerely,

Veronica Valentine

Editor, McGee Whitney Books for Young Readers

That should do the trick. I start a new email and copy the letter into it. But since this letter might help me nab a promotion, I'm going to treat it like soup. Let my words simmer a bit before I hit send.

I set aside questions of *oomph* and dramatic tension between Frog and Prince and log in to my personal email. Scrolling through my messages, I save one from Peace of Cake about the new vanilla celebration special, and then I star a note from Just for Her advertising twenty percent off on its newest toy, The Wave 2.0, powered by sonic waves. Ooh, baby. Imma gonna need that too. Since The Wave 1.0 was a ten out of ten I'd use it again.

I'm about to close out when I spot a note from Bellamy Hart, who oversees my anonymous column at The Dating Pool. I open it at cheetah speed.

Love the ideas for your next column, V. I'm open to either "How to Break the News to Your Date" or "Assumptions People Make about Virgins." I favor the latter, but I'm good with both. Let the muse decide. Can you send it in tomorrow morning so I can run it in the evening, as per usual?

Can I send it tomorrow? *Please.* How about tonight, Bellamy? Time to impress her too.

Especially since my mind is already wandering from thoughts of princes and frogs to other things that could be teased.

Like, say, *me*, by Mister Sexy Pants.

While StudMuffin adjusts himself into a tighter dog ball in his bed, my monster-sized Siamese leaps onto my lap. I meet his pretty blue eyes. "Which topic do you like better, Hot Stuff?"

As I stroke his soft fur, thoughts of the frog and the prince melt away entirely, replaced by vivid images of a man in tight pants, displaying a chivalry you rarely see anymore.

That run-in this afternoon did nothing to douse my crush after that fun, flirty convo from the cake shop a few months ago. Meeting him again today stoked the flames, thanks to his reaction. Most men would have scowled, reprimanded me, and rode off. I can't stand rudeness. I went on a date two weeks ago with a musician who showed up twenty-five minutes late and he didn't even apologize. But he's a knight in shining armor compared to the guy I had dinner with a month ago. When the smoke detector at the restaurant bleeped during dinner, my date darted up, and rushed out first, pushing other diners aside like his pants were on fire.

So the chivalry of my main crush picking up my glitter tube when my dog wanted to devour his bicycle is delectable.

I step away from the table, set Hot Stuff down, weave through the tiny living room, then push open the doors to my balcony, drawing a deep inhale of the herby scent of rosemary and sage, kale and pole beans from the miniature garden. As I stare down at the scene of the glitter crime, words and ideas snap into place.

I replay the moment once again and imagine a new ending.

Then I open my dictation app and pace the tiny width of my balcony, talking into the phone as my next column takes shape.

Things We Assume About Virgins

I've never flown on a private jet with cushy leather seats and world-class service. Nor have I spent an evening in a penthouse hotel suite with a view of the Seine.

Likewise, I've never banged on a balcony.

Yet I can say with one hundred percent certainty I'd enjoy the hell out of zooming through the sky at thirty thousand feet, savoring strawberries and champagne, and reclining all the way in the leather seats. (Note: it's my fantasy so the seats are magically made of vegan leather.)

After my flight, I'd relish sweeping into my deluxe accommodation and sinking onto the soft, king-size bed overlooking the Seine.

I bet you're sure you'd love to travel like that too, even if you never have.

So why the hell does the world think a virgin doesn't know what she wants in bed?

I've never had sex, but I sure as hell have fantasies. Oh boy, do I ever have them.

Do you remember Mister Sexy Pants? I mentioned him a few weeks ago when he introduced me to the pleasures of ogling men in tight pants.

Today, I finally spoke to him again. And even though my valiant dog tried to defend me against a potential attack from his bike, and even though I accidentally flashed him my panties, he was still a perfect gentleman.

Which only gets me going more.

So now, I have a brand-new fantasy. Here goes.

I'm home, standing in front of the mirror, slicking on lipstick, when a text lands from Mister Sexy Pants. *Hey, Sweet Cheeks, I'm on my way home from work.* (Sidenote: Again, this is my fantasy, so he owns a combination bookstore and calorie-free cake shop. He's good with his hands too. Obvs.) When he comes home from work, he spots the broken sink, but then calls out to me, "I'll fix the broken pipe later. You come first, sunshine."

"And you mean that literally," I say, then I blow him a red-lipsticked kiss and sashay to the balcony. He follows me and I grab a handful of his shirt.

Wait. Nope.

In my fantasy, he's already stripped off the shirt so I'm free to roam my adventurous hands across his firm pecs, then over the grooves of his abs.

I let go, spin around, and lift my skirt, giving him a peek of my come-and-get-me undies.

He growls with desire, then bends me over the railing. As he kisses the back of my neck, he whispers the sexiest words ever: "I'm going to give you a knee-weakening, toe-curling orgasm, then make you a panini."

Gah. I am fanning myself right now.

So yeah, I'm here to tell you that a virgin can know what she wants even if she's never had sex.

I have an active imagination and I'm not afraid to use it.

Nor should you be.

Fantasies let us explore who we are and what we want. There's nothing wrong with taking some for a test drive together with a partner. Or alone with your mind. Just make sure you have enough batteries.

And don't ever be ashamed of your dirty dreams.

I hit stop, then shake my booty. Whew. That felt damn good.

I hit transcribe on the audio file and head inside to edit and clean up the column. When I'm done, I read it again, pleased with this newest installment.

After one final read, I open an email to Bellamy and drop in the fabulous words. Then, as I let it simmer for a few, I jam through my work emails, fingers flying, hitting new productivity heights. Yes! This is how I'm making up for my mishap. With focused, diligent work. Maybe I did make lemonade today after all.

I step away to make a cup of chai to power me through the rest of my list.

When I return to the table, I set down the tea as Hot Stuff jumps from the couch onto the table. I grab for the cup, but he's faster, skidding into it.

I yank it as far away from the keyboard as possible, the liquid sloshing onto the table rather than the machine.

Whew. That was close.

"Hot Stuff," I mumble as I trot to the kitchen to grab a towel.

As I clean up the table, Hot Stuff parks himself next to my laptop, licking chai off his paw while giving me the evil eye.

"Yes, that was all *my* fault," I say, flopping back down on the chair to finalize the work email as the light streaming through the window turns golden. Hmm. It's evening now. No one in publishing likes getting work emails at this hour, but Bellamy is a night owl. I fire off the column to her and make a note to double check my editorial letter to Agnes in the morning, then send it when people are arriving at work.

I shower, dry my hair, and pop next door to order takeout Thai with my friend Ellie. When the food arrives, we hunker onto her purple couch with the pad thai and eggplant tofu and place bets on who'll hook up in this episode of *A Gentleman's Deal.*

My Spidey sense for canoodling is on point.

"You win." Ellie pouts at the end.

"Which means you pay for takeout next week," I say.

"As if I don't know the rules," she says.

When I return to my apartment, I contemplate taking up Just for Her on the offer, but I'll deal with that tomorrow.

* * *

In the morning, I wake up to kisses on my nose, so I hop out of bed, tug on workout clothes, and grab my phone.

My notifications are lit up, but that's par for the course.

I'll enjoy a quick walk, then dive straight into work mode and take care of all these pesky emails.

I'm properly dressed as I leave home. What an accomplishment.

4

A DEADLY GAME OF FROGGER

Milo

As the sun peeks over the horizon, I'm walking up Hudson Street, Trudy trotting happily by my side.

Finally, *fucking finally*, mornings shine again.

I'm talking to my brother on the phone, updating him on yesterday's dog-for-dough exchange. "And then I signed the check," I finish.

Bryan whistles in begrudging admiration. "Damn, that is some slick work on Callie's part."

"Yes, please laud my ex's talents a little more," I say drily, slowing for Trudy to sniff the step of a locksmith's shop.

"That's not what I meant. Some people say they have the worst ex, but you truly do. She is the literal worst. You could write one of those columns for BuzzFeed or HuffPost on being hoodwinked by online dating," he points out, trying to be helpful. "So other guys can be on the lookout."

I get where he's coming from, but no effing way. "That's a hard pass on telling the world how I was suckered," I say, shuddering. Dating is a game of Frogger where everyone dies. That's the only useful piece of advice I'd have to share. "I'm still on a dating info blackout. No writing about it; no reading about it. That shit stresses me out. I'm trying to build my business, not develop an ulcer at age twenty-nine."

"I hear ya," he says. "Best to put the whole Callie mess behind you and look forward."

"That's the plan." But focusing on business won't be easy. I'm out five grand and rent is insane at my combo bike/flower shop in the Village. I've got to find a way to market Bikes and Blooms more, especially since competition is getting tougher on both sides of the business, and my flower shop manager is about to go on maternity leave. I have a new hire to take care of too. I really could have used those five big bills for new online ads. But when I tug the leash gently and Trudy turns her sweet face up at me, I try not to worry. "All worth it though for my girl."

We walk on.

"You and your dog," Bryan says. "And let's keep it that way for now, okay?"

He's preaching to the choir. "Yup, it's just Trudy and . . ."

My pulse picks up as I catch a glimpse of chestnut hair and a cute figure.

Whoa. Is that who I think it is?

I'm momentarily distracted by yoga pants and fate.

Glitter Gal just crossed the street up ahead, and now she's walking her tiny blond monster thirty or so feet in front of me. What are the chances? Well, okay, she lives on Grove, so the chances aren't that slim.

"You still there, Milo?" Bryan asks.

Busted. But in my defense, Glitter Gal is wearing pink yoga pants, and her hair is swept up in a bouncy ponytail.

"Yeah, but yoga pants," I say stupidly, trying to explain my temporary loss of power.

"English, please."

I drop my voice; I don't want all of New York to know I'm the horndog who ogles his neighbor. Just my brother gets that intel. "The woman in front of me is wearing tight pink workout pants. I ran into her yesterday, and a few months before that, and she's fucking adorable and has these skull earrings I need to return to her. Oh, and Miss Yoga Pants has a dog too," I babble as I pass an organic dry cleaner, doing my best to stop gawking at the brunette.

I'm failing miserably, though, but my eyes are so damn happy right now.

"Milo," Bryan growls, like only an older brother can. "Get it together, man. Didn't you just say you're not dating?"

I straighten my spine. Yeah, I did. Shit. I need to act like it. "I'm *not* dating," I say, defending myself. "I'm *staring* like the pig I am."

"If the oink fits." Then his tone shifts to serious. "You don't need any more trouble in your life right now."

I nod like that'll reinforce the point. He's so damn right. "Yup. I'll just return her earrings, then I'll be on my way."

"Be careful," he warns.

"I will," I say, then hang up.

I'm simply going to be the ombudsman at the Neighborhood Department of Lost and Found. That's the right thing to do. The earrings are upstairs in my apartment, so once I catch up to her, I'll get her name and number, and then drop them off later.

Wait. I won't even get her number. Just her name. I can be good. I'm like Trudy—highly trainable.

She rounds the corner onto Grove Street, and I pick up the pace so I can catch up to her before she reaches her door. I turn onto the same block, Trudy and I race-walking till Glitter Gal is ten, five, three feet in front. "Hey there," I call out.

She wheels around, arms raised instantly in some sort of self-defense move, leash curled around her wrist. Her dog chirps at me, shouting dog obscenities.

"Whoa," I say immediately, lifting my hands in surrender.

With a relieved sigh, she lowers her hands. "It's *you*. Whew. You just never know." She blinks, then smiles. Damn, she really is pretty with those freckles and those bright green eyes. Shifting her attention to the little guy, she coos to him, "It's fine, honey."

He stops barking.

"Yeah, it's just . . . *me*," I say, as Trudy whines excitedly, then sniffs at the littler dog as they scope each other out.

The brunette points at my beard. "You're no longer a leprechaun."

"Soap. It works wonders."

Pressing a hand to her chest, she says, "I *too* love soap." Then her focus drifts down to my pup. "And you have a dog, I see."

I beam. "That's Trudy. She's all mine, and she's very, very friendly," I say, as Trudy makes an honest man of me by going full downward dog mode to say hi to the other pup.

"Mine is StudMuffin," she says.

"What?" I ask, strangling the word.

"He's StudMuffin," she repeats.

Oh, man. I'm an idiot. "You said that yesterday and I thought—"

Her smile stretches. "You thought I was calling you StudMuffin?"

"Let's pretend I didn't even suggest that," I say.

Of course she didn't call you Stud Muffin. That's not a thing people do. Callie did such a number on you that you don't even know how normal convos with women work.

I choose an easier topic for conversation, rather than segueing straight into "So, I kidnapped your earrings" and appearing even stranger than I already have. Since the pooches are wound up in a sniffing circle, I point to them. "Your dog is less incensed today."

Glitter Gal's lips curve up. "He's only enraged by bikes, skateboards, and scooters. But bikes infuriate him the most."

"Cabs, buses, and trucks are my enemy when I'm riding a bike, so I do understand having a hit list," I say.

She laughs. Yes! This is it. The perfect opportunity.

"By the way, do you have skull—"

A foghorn blares from her phone and I grimace while she winces. That is the most obnoxious sound I've ever heard.

"That's my sister," she whispers heavily, as if her sister is summoning her to the underworld. "It's her emergency ring. I have to go."

"I hope everything's okay," I say, but she's answered the phone and is walking toward her stoop. I try not to eavesdrop, but I can't help but pick up the tail end of her conversation.

She freezes.

"For real? She said that online?" And she sounds horrified as she continues up the steps like she's heading to the guillotine. "Are you serious?"

A pause, and her steps falter. "Oh, god. I must have . . . Oh no . . . I can't believe I sent *that* to her."

Shit, someone is having a bad day.

Maybe the earrings will cheer her up. But I can do one better. I can fix them for her, and perhaps that'll be the pick-me-up she needs. Then, I'll leave them on her stoop and be on my way.

I have problems of my own, and none of them will be solved by trying to engineer another flirting session.

I just wish she weren't so damn flirt-worthy.

5

———

THE SEX AND SANDWICHES
GIVEAWAY

Veronica

I'm shaking with embarrassment as I shut the door of my apartment and sink to the floor.

"I thought it might be you when I saw the sex and sandwiches post from Agnes."

"Yeah, kind of a giveaway, I'm the culprit."

"But at least it's not trending," Hazel says, trying to make the best of my blunder.

"I'm such an idiot," I mutter.

"No, you're not. We'll find a way to fix this. We always do," she says, eager to flex her big sister problem-solving muscles, and they're buff and toned for sure.

Only, I don't know if anyone can repair this damage.

"Thanks, Hazel," I choke out, pushing past the knot in my throat as I hang up and brace myself for all kinds of backlash.

While StudMuffin wanders to his water dish, I peek at my work email on my phone, then jerk away, gasping in terror. No wonder there were so many messages blinking at me when I got out of bed.

Not only did I send my *Virgin Club* column to Bellamy last night, I also, evidently, sent my bang-me-on-the-balcony fantasy to the entire distribution list at McGee Whitney Books, and to one very old-fashioned author, who was CC'ed too.

How the hell did this happen?

Heading to my laptop at the table, I try to retrace my steps from yesterday. I finished the editorial letter, opened the email to my company, then hit pause. I went to my deck, dictated *The Virgin Club* column, then when I got it back and edited it, I must have . . .

I groan.

When I copied my anonymous sex column, I must have hit paste in two places—once to Bellamy and once to everyone at work, copying on top of the editorial letter I'd meant to send.

But I didn't hit send on the Agnes letter. So how the hell is this damning mixed-up email in my sent messages?

Wishing terribly for that time machine once more, I glance up from the screen as Hot Stuff saunters out of the bathroom and heads my way, looking thoroughly innocent.

But also . . . *not?*

Oh, god. When he jumped on the keyboard last night, he must have fired off my email to McGee Whitney Books—the one I was saving to re-read in the morning. "Why are you such a cat?" I ask, annoyed at the critter.

But immediately, I feel terrible for lashing out at him. I reach down and haul his burly body into my lap. It's not his fault. I foolishly pasted the wrong contents. He just pulled the trigger with his big paws.

Shame engulfs me as I peer at the damage. Email after email from colleagues, from graphic designers, and from my boss asking me to meet her at eight-thirty in her office, even though we don't open till nine, then one from Twitter.

Why is Twitter emailing me?

The only reason is a possible alert. I set some up to track if my authors trend.

The hair on the back of my neck prickles.

No. Say it isn't so.

Agnes Millicent's post—the one Hazel spotted this morning—is now trending on Twitter. I want to crawl under the covers for the rest of time. But I have to look at the ten-car pileup that's my career.

I click over to the Internet's roasting pit, and I recoil as my career goes up in flames.

A lady never names names, so I won't divulge the perpetrator, but I cannot fathom why I received a tawdry letter this morning from McGee Whitney Books. A lewd, crude, and filthy email about sex and sandwiches. I am so very triggered. Might there be any other publishing house looking for an author who's sold millions of books for innocent children?

"There's nothing wrong with sex and sandwiches," I shout into the void. But there's no way to make lemonade of these lemons.

* * *

A few minutes later, I've taken the first step to fixing my error—I've sent the correct editorial letter to Blanche. Then I get dressed quickly, swipe on blush and lip gloss, and bang on Ellie's door. I warned her via text I was coming. No way am I heading into the lion's den of the office without her eyes checking me out from stem to stern. My judgment is a snake, and I don't trust it.

When she swings open the door, I gesture to my black slacks and black blouse. This close to hyperventilating, I blurt out: "Does this outfit say fire me on sight, or slap me on the wrist and let me off with a reprimand because I'm such an amazing editor and you can't bear to let me go?"

I press my palms together in prayer as Ellie gives me a serious once-over, then renders the verdict: "It says *I'm dressed for my own funeral.*"

Ugh. "I don't want to give them ideas." I lean my forehead against the doorjamb and moan into the wood. "Why can't she just fire me over email like a normal person who hates conflict would do?"

"Or via a text," Ellie says sympathetically.

"Maybe it's a good sign she called me in before the office opens—the perfect time for a reprimand and a talking-to before I go about my day?" I ask, my voice pitching up with hope.

"Yes! So put on your hot pink cap-sleeve blouse rather than your widow garb. Think positive thoughts," Ellie says, shooing me back to my apartment. She's such an upbeat person. Maybe some of it will rub off on me.

"Do you want me to watch StudMuffin? I have a table read this afternoon for *Unfinished Business,* but that's it. He can hang out with Gigi McDoodle and me till then, and maybe it'll just be a normal day at work for you."

I adore her optimism. No matter what happens in the office, at least I have good friends. "I would love that."

I pop back into my place to change my shirt and grab my little love. Back at Ellie's door, I give Stud-Muffin a firm squeeze, then hand him over and head out.

For the first time in a long time, I send a wish to the universe that I don't run into Mister Sexy Pants on the way to the office.

The universe delivers that small blessing.

6

THE PERPETRATOR

Veronica

Twenty minutes and one subway ride later, I arrive at the towering building in Midtown. Above the big brass doors is an illustration of a child reading a book while sitting on the moon, and I stare at it a moment while I gather my nerve.

You can do this.

My shirt's buttoned, pants are smoothed out after the subway ride, and nothing's stuck to the bottom of my shoes.

Check. So I swallow some courage and go inside, prepared to apologize profusely then take my punishment.

When I reach the eighth floor, it's church quiet, but it's early. The receptionist isn't even here yet. Swiping my card key, I push open the glass doors, and weave through mostly empty cubicles.

I'm halfway to Blanche's corner office when I hear a chair roll across the carpet and a baby-faced man sticks his head out of a cubicle. Darius Daniels—of course he's here. Spoiler alert: his chances of nabbing that promotion skyrocketed this morning.

"Hey, Veronica. You're in early today," he says, all chipper and pretend clueless, like he didn't read my fantasies about Mister Sexy Pants.

"Early bird and all," I say, not in the mood for small talk.

"Hope you get the worm," he says with a too-big grin, then rolls back to his desk in his chair, his lips twitching in a grin.

I continue down the hall where Blanche waits at the door. "Thanks for coming in early," she says, giving me a kind smile. I don't know if that makes me feel better or worse.

"Of course. Anytime," I say, nerves coiling inside me.

Blanche snicks the door shut, then gestures to a soft green chair in the seating area in front of her desk. I take it, and she sits across from me. Her red cat's-eye glasses reflect me and my tilt-a-whirl of emotions.

Before she can start, I own my mistake. Maybe I can get ahead of trouble with my atonement. "Whatever you need me to do to make up for this, I will. I want to make this right. I'm so sorry about the mix-up, but I hope the editorial letter impresses you and Miss Millicent."

Blanche is quiet for a long, weighty pause, fighting with an errant strand of blonde hair that's fallen from her French twist. "Veronica," she says heavily, and my shoulders fall. Her tone is all I need to know. "You're a wonderfully talented editor and I've loved working with you . . ."

Don't cry.

The entire company has read my dirty daydreams. They don't get to witness my real tears.

"I've loved working with you, Blanche," I say, taking time with each word so I don't fall to pieces.

"But we just lost one of our biggest writers because of this mix-up," Blanche says, and there's pain in her voice. Regret too. "I wish I didn't have to do this, but the decision came from the top."

I grimace but keep my chin up and my big girl panties on. "I should have been more careful. I should have checked the email before—"

I swallow *"my cat jumped on the keyboard."* No one wants to hear the dog-ate-my-homework excuse.

"Things happen with email," she says. "Sometimes I wish we didn't live in a digital age. In any case, I called you in so you can collect your things. And because it's easier to say this than to write this. We won't share your name as *the perpetrator*."

While that's a relief, secrecy is a small consolation. Now the entire company knows my hymen's intact, I'm horny for my next-door neighbor, and I regularly chronicle my imaginary sex-ploits for The Dating Pool. Gossip is the tastiest treat in the publishing business, and by lunch, everyone will be dining on news of my secret identity. Will I ever get another job in the industry again?

"Thank you," I say, keeping a stiff upper lip.

"We don't want to fan these flames," Blanche says,

"so we've instructed the entire company that this incident falls under the purview of the non-disclosure agreements they signed upon hiring, and disciplinary action may follow if they disclose details anywhere or to anyone."

Oh!

McGee Whitney Books really wants to bury this story, which might work in my favor if I ever want to work in children's publishing again.

"I appreciate that so much," I say, clinging to that spark of hope.

Blanche stands, indicating the meeting is over. Thanking her, I follow suit, then head for the door.

She clears her throat. "For what it's worth, I hope everything works out with Mister Sexy Pants and that whoever you meant to send that saucy letter to gets it after all."

Hold the presses.

That spark of hope ignites into fireworks. McGee Whitney Books doesn't know I write a column on sex and virginity? They just think I mistakenly sent them a raunchy letter meant for . . . a friend?

Oh. My. God.

Of course they think that. I didn't include in my email the name of my column, *The Virgin Club,* or my sign-off, *Your Friendly Neighborhood Virgin*, because those are automatically added in The Dating Pool system.

And if Agnes won't name names, then maybe, just maybe, the small world of publishing won't know Veronica Valentine is the sex and sandwich editor.

As long as the column doesn't run.

I'll have to call Bellamy as soon as I leave and ask her to kill the piece. I'll send her a replacement column, stat. I have all day to write a new one and still meet her evening publishing deadline.

Turning around to face Blanche, I mime zipping my lips. "I promise I won't say a word either," I say, then I grab the knob so I can hightail it out of here and alert Bellamy.

"And, um, one more thing." Blanche's pale cheeks pinken. "I was wondering if you had any tips on great, um, battery-operated friends?"

I didn't know what would happen when I came in today, but my boss asking me for a vibrator recommendation definitely wasn't in the running.

But I did say I'd do anything, so perhaps this is the start of my penance. "Just for Her has some excellent toys," I say warmly.

Blanche fidgets with that naughty hair strand again, then shifts her gaze around the room. "Anything for women who have a hard time . . . ahem . . . finishing?"

That makes me sad. I hate to hear when a lady can't get her O on. "Try Just for Her's The Wave. It's powered by sonic waves and it's life-changing," I say, happy to help.

She blinks. "Oh. I had no idea."

"Worth every penny."

"Thanks," she says, still flustered, but she lets go of that strand of hair at last. "And good luck. I'll write you a letter of recommendation and we won't mention this, um, incident."

"Thanks and good luck with . . ." *With your masturbation pursuits?*

I keep those parting words to myself as I rush to my former office, scoop up my framed pictures and signed books, and drop them into a canvas bag. I take off for the elevators at escape-from-a-lava-pit speed, stabbing the down button like I'm rushing into the ER on a hospital drama.

Once the doors open, I dart inside, and look up Bellamy's contact info. Finger hovering, I'm poised, ready to call the second the elevator frees me at the lobby.

When I reach the ground floor, I hit dial.

"Answer, please answer," I beg as I head to the exit while the phone rings and rings and rings.

On the fifth ring, she picks up. "Hey, Veronica. I'm heading to a meeting, but I saw you were calling. Your column is amazeballs," she says, and that is awesome news.

Except . . . not.

"I'm glad you like it," I say, as the revolving doors spit me out onto the busy avenue. "Though, I would love to send you a new one this afternoon on a new topic. I can explain why later, but you'll have a fresh, fantastic column for tonight."

Please say yes.

"Oh," she says, and I hear the let-down in her voice. "I would love to help. But it was so damn good, I made it go live early. It's your best column ever and it's already heating up. The Internet loves it."

All hope withers, right along with my fighting chance.

* * *

Wallowing sounds like the perfect prescription. Give me a glass of cheap Chardonnay, a couple of buckets of salted caramel anything, and the next season of *Lords and Ladies*, and I will gladly hunker down for the night.

But Ellie and Hazel won't let me. My sister calls an emergency meeting through our group chat and arrives that evening with a chanterelle and kale pizza, while Ellie brings her homemade seven-layer bar brownies. I've already started on the wine. Because . . . priorities.

"Hi, and welcome to my funeral," I say as I open the door. The wine sloshes in the glass as I sweep my arm to invite them into my pity party, but it doesn't spill. "Who wants first stab at the eulogy?"

Hazel wags a chiding finger in my face. "Nope, we have plans."

"And they all involve life after publishing," Ellie puts in, as StudMuffin whines a happy hello in greeting. He loves his ladies.

With my free hand, I snag the pizza box and carry it to the table. "I'd rather have pizza," I say, then fold a slice and chew, letting the drugs of carbs and cheese numb the pain of the day.

It's too hard for me to imagine life after publishing. As a kid, I devoured books like I'm devouring this pizza. All I've ever wanted to do was edit children's books like the ones I stayed up reading past my bedtime. Now my dreams are roadkill, so I stuff more pizza into my mouth.

Hazel grabs a chair and reaches into her cavernous purse. Fishing out a notebook, she slaps it down on the table.

Ellie takes a seat too and drops a handful of purple, pink, and green gel pens on the table.

Plink, plink, plink.

I moan in misery. I love notebooks and colorful pens, especially for the start of my editorial letters. "Did you come to torture me about my anti-future in publishing?"

Hazel shakes her head, adamant. "You do have a future in publishing. Because what does publishing love most of all?"

"Thrillers with bad sex scenes written by men who get paid more than women?"

"Well, yes. But also a redemption story," Hazel says as my dog curls up at her feet.

Ellie waves imaginary pom-poms. "And that'll be you in a few months. Everything dies down eventually," she says. "No scandal lasts forever. Isn't that what the last season of *Lords and Ladies* taught us? Even after Frederick was jilted on his wedding day, and no one would go near him, he still found a happy ending."

"But that's, ahem, fiction. And I don't have the luxury of time," I point out.

Hazel grins, patting the notebook and pens. "That's why you're going to find a temporary job this summer. We're going to make a list of your skills. As long as you don't start looking for a new publishing job right this second, while people can put two and two together and figure out that you're *the perpetrator*, you have a shot at coming back. You need to lie low for a month or two and then start working on your triumphant return. I'll talk to my editor in the meantime. I'll ask friends too. I will do whatever recon I can."

It's not a bad argument. Scandals lose their luster. Maybe I can hunt for a job editing children's books at the end of the summer.

And, as I glance at my sleeping pup, I hit reverse on my wallowing course. I've got a dog to feed, a cat to take care of, bills to pay, and, hello, undies and toys to buy.

Also, I hate wallowing. I'm remarkably bad at it because there's too much I like doing. I like gardening, and animals, and friends. I like exploring New York, and talking to people, and consuming stories.

And I really like making lists too.

As we eat and drink, I inventory my skills from teaching art to kids, to whipping up an excellent mojito. Not to mention my talent for growing kale like the badass balcony gardener that I am. And then there's my niche talent for writing about dating and virginity.

When we're done with the list, I start to see possibilities. Freelance editing, tutoring, art teacher, social media maven. "If anyone needs a sex toy tester, I'd be in high demand," I say, because talk about a dream job . . .

"Oh! What about your column?" Ellie asks hopefully.

I smile sadly, shaking my head. "I mostly do it for fun. It pays peanuts, as most columns do. I can't live on it."

Even though my job died because of it.

I've spent the day checking social media, and so far, no one has connected the dots between Mister Sexy Pants in my letter and Mister Sexy Pants in *The Virgin Club* column.

Maybe Blanche's email warning did the trick.

And maybe the readership of The Dating Pool and the ranks of my former colleagues don't overlap. Whatever the reason, I'll take it, thank you very much.

"Then let's find some jobs you *can* live on. You need more side hustles," Ellie says. "That's why I do voiceover work. It pays the bills in between the rare TV and movie gigs."

"Ellie, you're a regular on a hit TV show," I point out.

"And it could get canceled at any minute, so side hustles matter," she says, her gaze wandering to the deck outside the patio door, then landing on the rosemary and the sage. With a glimmer in her brown eyes, she returns her focus to me. "You know, I have a friend who runs a cute shop that might need your balcony gardening skills. Let me make some calls tomorrow."

"That would be great," I say.

When they leave at the end of the night, I steal one final peek at the column, scanning some comments.

Stocked up on batteries!

Long live dirty dreams.

I recommend mac and cheese after sex.

That does sound yummy. But first, I need a job. A girl's got to have priorities. First, rent, then shtupping.

I get ready for bed and am sliding under the covers

to read on my phone when an email lands from Bellamy. *Most popular piece of the day! Keep 'em coming.*

At least there's one company in New York that wants a piece of me.

That's a start, and I need all the new beginnings I can get.

7

BIG DICTIONARIES

Milo

The store is closed and quiet on Thursday night. But here in the back, I'm blasting the *Science is Sexy* podcast under the bright fluorescents as I put the finishing touches on a complicated bike repair I've been working on all week.

And . . . done.

I take off the glasses I wear for up-close work and tuck them into my pocket. Stretching my neck from side to side, I spin the pedals on the bike. "Check this out, girl," I say to Trudy, who's snoozing at my feet.

She lifts her snout.

"I know. You're impressed with my skills," I say. Me too, since this bike is for a pro cyclist, and he'll be stoked to have his wheels back in time for a big race.

With that finished at last, I grab the skull earring from the workbench and quickly fix the hook. I drop the earrings into a small envelope. I'll leave it on Glitter Gal's stoop on the way home, except I don't know her name.

Trudy pops up, then stretches into a downward dog. Thank you, girl. I know her dog's name. On the front of the envelope, I write: *For StudMuffin.*

I snag a piece of paper from a pad on the counter, then scribble out a note to leave inside.

Hey, you! I found your earrings the other day. At least, I think they're yours. One of the hooks was missing so I fixed it. Hope your day got better.
Me ☺
(Or you can call me Glitter Beard)

I head home, scanning up and down our block in case she's walking her little dog.

No such luck, but I'm not angling for another fun and flirty conversation with her, so it's no biggie. I bound up her steps.

Before I leave the envelope, though, I impulsively grab a pen from my backpack and write my number on the bottom of the note. She might want to say thanks. I'd be a dick if I deprived her of that chance.

Then, I head home.

Tomorrow is a big day for Bikes and Blooms. I need to get cracking on a new hire that's bedeviled me. I should have done it a month ago, but I was too caught up in the dog custody thing. Now that I've got Trudy back in my life, I can move forward on taking care of my business.

* * *

On Friday morning, as Trudy and I head to work, I cast a glance at Glitter Gal's brick building. The envelope is gone. That's good.

I check my phone.

My texts are empty. That's a shame.

But I refuse to think about the woman. Nothing will get in the way of my plans today.

Fifteen minutes later, I push on the door to Bikes and Blooms and head inside. Trudy scampers in ahead of me, trotting like a sassy miniature pony.

Waif-like Zara pops up from the bike she's tuning, then beams as she sets down her wrench. "Girly girl," she calls out, stretching out her inked arms to invite Trudy in for a hug.

Eager for puppy cuddles too, my pregnant friend Iris ambles around the dahlia display, cooing sweetly, "I have a biscuit for the good girl."

"No fair," Zara shouts, as Trudy does what a dog does—follows the food.

Iris shrugs innocently, beckoning my girl with a treat. "When we bet who she'd greet first, we never said anything about secret advantages."

"I didn't think we had to," Zara huffs, dark eyes crinkling against her olive skin.

I watch with amusement as I wheel my bike behind

the counter, then set my helmet and Trudy's on a shelf. It's good to be back to business as usual, my dog and me at work thirty minutes before we open.

Trudy wags her butt and takes the treat from Iris. "I'm going to miss you the most," Iris says to the dog.

"Am I chopped liver?" I ask. "We've only been friends since college."

Iris stands, ambles over to me, and squeezes my shoulder. "I can't miss you if you don't let me go."

"Today, I swear," I say, stabbing the bike counter for emphasis. "We are hiring your replacement today, Iris. No matter how many times I try to nix your newest choice."

Iris arches a brow. "You mean it, Mister Picky? You've eighty-sixed everyone I've brought you so far. Are you really going to follow through on hiring a new flower shop manager today?"

I hold up my right hand. "You have my word. We're going to find someone fantastic to fill in for you this summer."

While I *have* been distracted recently, the candidates so far have been all wrong. One guy had a perma-scowl. Another checked her Instagram three times during the interview. Yet another asked for a nap cot. As an employer, the participation trophy generation drives me a little bananas. "I will not leave till we have your replacement," I say.

Iris smiles. "Actually, my friend Ellie has the perfect person. She has a good friend who's—in her words—whip smart, outgoing, great with people, and has crazy knowledge about flowers. Her name is Veronica and we spoke on the phone yesterday. I'm interviewing her at eleven today in the shop."

That sounds promising. "I have a call with one of my regular parts suppliers for my new custom design. But I should be done by eleven-fifteen. You can get started and I'll join you," I say, hoping this Veronica person will be the answer to my biggest business problem.

I head to my small office in the back and settle in at the computer to tackle billing and invoices. Trudy follows, curling up on the carpet.

A few minutes later, my phone buzzes with a text.

When I see a 917 number I don't recognize, I feel a little fizzy.

You. Fixed. My. Earring. You deserve cake AND beer for this. Thank you so much.

The fizz expands like bubbles as I hit reply. ***That sounds like a perfect combination for . . . anytime. Glad you got the earrings.***

There. I'm just being a good guy. That's all. I set the phone down, but it pings again. ***I'd been meaning to get a new hook, but life kept happening, then, well, you did THIS. You're a superhero.***

Best compliment ever. ***It was easy. I was happy to do it. And you seemed like you needed a Good Samaritan in your life.***

Before I can even think about returning to invoices, the phone vibrates again. Fine, fine, I get it. I'm irresistible. I click open her new message, giving her a name in my texts, then reading.

Miss Cute Devil Butt: I would ask if it was that obvious I needed help, but I know it was that obvious I needed help. This is a week of pure I-can't-even-ing. But these earrings take away some of the sting. I'm going to wear them to an appointment this morning. For luck!

See? Maybe some guys Callie dated hate me and think I hoodwinked them, but this sweetheart of a woman thinks I'm a rock star. And, well, it was fun to help her. I write back.

Milo: Nice work turning 'I can't even' into a gerund.

Miss Cute Devil Butt: Gah. First soap, now grammar. I, too, love grammar.

I haven't laughed like this in a long time. I should get back to the invoices, but I allow myself one more text exchange.

Milo: I had a feeling you liked grammar and words after you slid from enraged to infuriated when we were talking about your incensed dog.

Miss Cute Devil Butt: I like big vocabularies and I cannot lie.

Groaning, I lean back in my chair, dragging a hand across my chin. What am I doing? Exactly what I said I wouldn't—I said I wouldn't get distracted.

Helpless to the buzz building in me, I turn to Trudy for advice. She's watching me with her big brown eyes. "Girl, maybe I could ask her out on *one* date. That's all. No strings. What do you think?"

My pooch tilts her head to the side. She can't even believe I'm asking.

I hold up a hand in surrender. "Fine. I won't. I'll just text her one more time. Then, I'm done, I swear."

Milo: You know what they say about a man with a big vocabulary . . .

Miss Cute Devil Butt: No. Do tell.

Milo: He has a big dictionary.

I have work to do. I *should* get moving. But I'm too eager to hear back. I'll allow myself one last exchange, then I'll turn my phone to silent. And her response lands.

Miss Cute Devil Butt: That's a book you can read over, and over, and over . . .

I laugh out loud. She is too much. Would it really ruin my no-romance plan if I took her out for that cake and beer date? Followed by some sex and orgasms? I know she likes cake. I bet she loves orgasms. It'd be a perfect two-fer.

Then I'd be on my way.

She seems like she'd be cool with that scenario.

I'm considering the perfect reply, when Miss Cute Devil Butt texts me one more time with, *Gotta go. Thanks again.*

Okaaaay.

That's a buzzkill for ya. There will be no cake, beer, or coming.

8

———

MISTRESS OF CHEEK

Veronica

My mom is calling me back, so I jump away from the text string and swipe up on FaceTime, smiling nervously. She's the one I need to talk to, not that clever, thoroughly distracting man.

I've wanted to get to know him for a few months now, and at last, I am.

Finally, my crush is moving out of crush territory and into Maybe a Little More Land.

But first things first. I need Mom's help. "Hey, Mama Valentine. Would you hire me if I came into your store like this?"

I give her a ta-da pose in my living room. I'm wearing a cute summery dress with a daisy pattern on yellow fabric. The flower faces are winking, so that feels perfect. A little sassy. I looked up Bikes and Blooms on social, and the shop has a fun and irreverent vibe, though it could use a touch more cheek in its online presence.

What do you know? I'm the mistress of cheek, and I plan to arrive at the interview armed and ready with new material for the store's social media.

As Mom ties the strings on her green apron, she gives me a quick once-over. "I'd probably make the decision based on your knowledge of plants, soil, and sun, as well as your personality, but sure, the dress is cute."

I huff. "Mom, I have all that. I'm *just* asking about the dress. Is it appropriate? You're an employer and all. Is this okay to wear to a job interview? I'm not the best judge."

"It's adorable and professional," she says thoughtfully, as she adds a bow in the middle of her apron. She'll be opening her garden shop any minute now.

"Thank you," I say, relieved. Someday, maybe even someday soon, I won't need all these wardrobe affirmations, but today is not that day. "Just think, at last, I can use all that flower and plant knowledge you drilled into my head growing up."

"Gee, hon. You make it sound so painful," she says, but I was only joking. Mom's ways of teaching were so much kinder than Dad's.

"Lovingly drilled?" I tease, as she moves down a row of plants and bushes. She's at her store in Wistful, Connecticut, the place she opened after spending years as a landscape architect designing gardens all over New England.

"I prefer to think of it as prepping you with useful

skills for a zombie apocalypse," she says.

"And I'm so grateful for that." I carry the phone out to my deck, swinging the lens to show off the kale I'm nurturing. "That's why I keep up my balcony garden. So I can trade herbs and kale during the end days. Poor Hazel though. She'll be eaten first. No one will need a romance novelist then."

"It's a shame, but the zombies will probably enjoy her brain, so there's that. And good luck today, sweetheart. You have a tasty brain too, and you can use it to impress the folks at the interview. I'm sure you'll wow them with your knowledge and charm," she says, and some days, she's such a mom.

But that's exactly why I called her. I'd never call my dad for advice. He'd tell me every error was my fault. I once said *I could care less,* and he made me write *I couldn't care less* one hundred times before dinner. "Thanks, Mama V. I needed that," I say.

After I hang up, I leash up my pooch for a quick walk around the hood. I've had a busy few days, life-hacking through joblessness Gen-Z style, posting freelance for hire signs all over the web.

So far, I've gotten nibbles on writing a training manual on keeping spiders as pets and editing a series of inspirational quotes on running, which I consider to be Satan's exercise.

But I'm keeping the faith that there's solid temporary work out there for me. Like this flower gig—the pay is decent, and the job is daily. It gives me time to stay off the radar and let the publishing world forget my faux pas.

As I walk down Eighth Avenue with my little dude sniffing the sidewalk, I click back to my texting app. Do I want to start up again with Mister Sexy Pants? Finding those earrings in the foyer—they were tacked up on the bulletin board with a note from the sweet lady in 2E who found them on the stoop—was an unexpected delight this morning.

The text exchange was the icing on the cake, and I can't stop smiling. Come to think of it, chatting with him put me in a damn good mood pre-interview. Might as well keep it up.

But as I contemplate what to say next, my phone trills with a call from Bellamy.

My shoulders tighten. She rarely calls. What if it's bad news? Like, the Internet figured out I'm the perpetrator and now all of kid lit has canceled me? This is the kind of week where birds poop on your head.

I answer right away, wary as hell. "Hi, Bellamy. Has anyone figured out who I am?" I ask quickly.

Bellamy was aware of my day job when she hired me. She's also a good friend of my sister's, and I trust her too, so she's been briefed on what went down.

"Nope! No one seems to have connected the Mister Sexy Pants in your column and the one in your, well, your work email. Ergo, you're still just *the friendly neighborhood virgin*, and no one's the wiser to your Clark Kent identity."

Yes! All the pooping pigeons in the city fly elsewhere. "Excellent. What can I do for you?" I ask.

"I'd normally email, but I figure when it involves money, a call is good," she says.

"I like money," I say as my pooch stops to whizz on a hydrant.

"And I like popular columns. So, we want to pay you a little extra since your column went viral. Readers are still having a blast speculating about who Mister Sexy Pants is," she says, sounding amused, and my cheeks heat just hearing his secret name. Maybe it won't be so secret much longer. "Some muse he's a bookstore owner, like you said," Bellamy continues as StudMuffin resumes his walk. "And they imagine he likes to read the dirty passages out loud to his lady. Others think he's a baker who licks frosting off spoons in a most sensual fashion, and a few imagine he's a carpenter, who sure knows how to hammer. But this is my favorite comment—*I bet he's a secret prince with a hidden library in his castle, but it's a library that doubles as a sex dungeon so he can read to you then spank you with the hardcover.*"

Damn. My *Virgin Club* readers have even dirtier minds than I do. "Sign me up. For all of those," I say as I turn the corner onto a quieter block.

Bellamy laughs. "I know, right? Readers love the mystery. Never underestimate the value of speculation."

I've been wondering too. Who *is* the man behind the texts? I never got his name the day I chatted with him over vanilla celebration cake. And I haven't asked his name yet. Maybe because I didn't want to break the spell of the flirting this morning. But for the longest time I've wondered who he is, and now I'm on the cusp of finding out.

It feels right.

Like it's finally time.

After the interview, I'm definitely going to ask his name. He's given me plenty of clues today that he's interested, including his very obvious *big dictionary* remark.

Yup, if I get the job, I'm going to reward myself by asking him out. Bet he tastes better than cake. A date will be a delicious end to the week from hell.

"I'm glad they're enjoying the column even more," I say, giving my full focus to Bellamy rather than my post-interview plans.

"They are. And we can pay a little extra if you can answer some questions from readers. You can do it on Twitter or Instagram. Whatever works for you, but there are all sorts of questions on your column, so it might be fun to interact with readers. I think it'll make the next one you write even more popular."

She gives me the amount, and it's coffee change, but I'll happily take it. "I'd love to. And what do you want for the next column?"

"Readers like your fantasy columns the best. I would love another one like that. Top ten things you want to do in bed would probably light up the socials."

It might light up my pants too. "I'm in," I say as I finish the call.

Then, I take my boy home and say goodbye to my pets.

It's time for the interview.

As I sail downstairs, I remind myself to rein in my sarcasm, my love of naughty puns, and, hmm, well now, anything about the ten things I want to do in bed.

Along the way to the flower shop, I review my

knowledge of tulips, lilies, peonies, then all the upcoming special occasions that call for flowers, then my ideas for catchy ways to promote florals as the perfect gift.

But as I head down Sixth Avenue, I feel a little unfinished. Maybe it's because of my last text with the guy who saved my lucky earrings.

I had to jump, and I might have left him hanging. That's not good if I plan to ask him out as my reward.

I'll just send one more quick message, maybe even tease at the whole *what's your name* thing. I click open the thread and type.

Veronica: By the way, now that I've learned you have jewelry-fixing skills, I think I'll call you Sir Good With His Hands.

But that's a little long for a name in my text app, so I decide to call him . . . well, *him*. He's the OG crush, after all, so it works.

As I turn onto Seventh Avenue, a text hits my phone.

Him: Was Sir Great With His Hands taken?

Veronica: 'Fraid so. You could be Sir Best With His Hands, but it just doesn't roll off the tongue the same way.

Him: Rolling off the tongue is important.

Gah. This is going so well. I can't wait to ask him out.

Veronica: It's truly a vital skill.

Him: One that must be practiced . . . daily.

I glance around the street like someone might see me blushing from the naughtiness on my phone. I want to fan myself, but maybe I shouldn't risk turning up the temperature before I interview for a job. Reluctantly, I shift gears.

Veronica: By the way, I'm wearing the earrings. I am feeling all the good luck vibes.

Him: Good. I hope your appointment goes well.

I wrack my brain for a response as I pass a cute coffee shop, but before I can compose one, three dots appear on the screen. Oh! He's a double texter. I might swoon right now.

. . .

Him: Incidentally, you have a nickname too.

Veronica: Don't keep it to yourself. Sharing is caring.

Him: It's not earth-shatteringly original, but it is apropos. Miss Cute Devil Butt ☺

I groan, but I'm laughing too as I write back.

Veronica: I will never live that down.

Him: Nor should you. Since there's no way I could ever forget the sight of your butt in those undies. It made my Monday.

I'm giddy as I near my destination. I'm officially sure Trudy's owner is into me too.

Veronica: You have to stop making me blush immediately. I have to do this job interview now, and I can't be thinking of The Day I Flashed Sir Greatest With His Hands.

Him: Greatest! I am the greatest and I can prove it! Let me know how your meeting goes. Can't wait to hear.

And yup . . . it's official. He wants to hear from me again, and he is indeed going to.

But I've turned onto the Bikes and Blooms block now, so I tuck my phone away. Two shops away, I stop in front of a chichi boutique and check my reflection.

All systems are go, so I walk a few more feet, open the green door to Bikes and Blooms, and stride inside, greeted by the fresh, sumptuous smell of flowers and bike grease.

Weirdly, the combo works.

The shop is mostly quiet, but I spot a pretty Black woman whose pregnant belly is the size of a house. She's chatting with a customer about sunflowers, so I busy myself, checking out the gift cards.

After the woman rings up the flowers, she works her way around the counter and comes up to me.

"You must be Veronica?" she asks.

"Veronica Valentine. It's a pleasure to meet you, Iris," I say, then extend my hand.

She shakes my hand and her head. "Veronica Valentine. That is not fair."

I messed up already? "What's not fair?" I ask nervously.

"I want your name," she says.

I laugh, relieved. "My parents were very good to me in the naming department," I say. "And you have a perfect name for a florist. Were you meant to be a florist, or did you pick your name?"

"I picked it. This was my dream—to open a flower shop. My best friend runs the business, and he wanted to start a bike shop, but I suggested flowers too, and he liked the idea. So he turned it into bikes and flowers so we could both have jobs."

"He sounds like a prince," I say, wondering if maybe he put the baby in her belly, friends-to-lovers style. I peer around the trendy space, admiring the lush green walls on the flower side, then the sky-blue ones on the bike half. A mint-green cruiser bike sits in between the two; the bike's basket filled with flowers. "I think the whole combo shop is perfect. It appeals to our go, go, go mentality, but it's got a touch of whimsy to it."

Iris's eyes twinkle like I said the perfect thing. "Yes, that's exactly the vibe we want to hit." She nods to the counter. "Let's chat more about your background, Veronica."

We talk at the counter while she tends to the occasional customer. In between, I answer her questions and tell her about my mother's work in gardens and how I grew up surrounded by flowers and plants.

"You graduated with a degree in English lit, though? And now, you're looking for a new job after working in publishing?" She's curious, but not cutting.

Still, an unpleasant knot tightens in my gut. I don't want to delve into my job history if I don't have to. "Yes, I'm looking into new things," I say.

"Fair enough," she says, and I'm glad she seems satisfied with that. "You know this is a temporary position for the summer? I'll return in three months." She pats her belly for emphasis.

"Which makes it perfect," I say, "since I have plans for the fall."

The more I say that, the more I'll believe it.

"Well, this seems almost too good to be true. I've been trying to find a replacement for some time," Iris says, with new excitement.

I can feel the offer coming when she swings her gaze to the door that leads to the back. "I think you'd be terrific, though I know Milo wants to meet you first. He's the owner," she explains.

"Wonderful," I say, with a smile fueled by fresh hope.

I hear the scritch of paws, then a hopeful whine. Seconds later, a brown and tan Min-Pin scurries around the corner through the flowers, beelining for me.

That dog is familiar.

That's . . .

"Trudy!" I call out and bend to the critter.

She runs straight to me like we're old friends, hopping up on her back legs and giving me kisses.

"You know Trudy?" Iris asks, delighted but curious.

Wait. Hold on. Why is Sir Great With His Hands' dog here?

When I untangle myself from Trudy and stand, I come face-to-face with the guy I want to date tonight.

How is this possible? Am I the butt of every joke in the city?

But nobody is laughing, least of all me.

9

———

MY HOT MESS WEEK

Veronica

Mister Sexy Pants blinks and then whispers a strangled, "You?"

"Me," I manage to choke out.

His chiseled, scruffy jaw is unhinged. "You're Veronica?"

I nod. "You're Milo?"

"Yes . . . that's some luck," he says in disbelief. But when Iris shoots him a *what's-going-on* look, he recovers. "I'm Milo Dawson, the owner of Bikes and Blooms," he says in a warm tone, but it's the professional kind of warm.

There is a flock of pigeons flying above the store, laughing at me, cackling, *"How do you like this pigeon poop now?"*

Somehow, I manage to sound composed. "Pleasure to meet you."

"And you," he says and extends a hand.

I take it, and yes, this is everything the handshake with the hot guy is supposed to be.

A little spark. A little sizzle. A magnetic charge.

The universe has one hell of a twisted sense of humor. I jerk my hand back so I don't yank him against me.

"So, you're applying for the florist manager job?" he asks, like he doesn't believe his bad luck either.

"And she's perfect for it," Iris cuts in, shooting her dazed boss a bewildered look. She goes over my background, punctuating each word like he's five and not getting it. She finishes with, "And you gave me your word you'd hire my replacement today. But you two can chat. I'm going to visit the little girl's room."

And I'm alone in the flower shop with the guy I spent the morning flirt-texting. The guy I was working up to asking out. The guy I wrote fantasies about and shared with my former employer and ALL OF THE WORLD.

This is the hottest mess of my hot-mess week.

There's no way I can take this job. That would be so awkward. He probably won't want to hire the gal he dirty flirted with either.

He fidgets with a potted flower on the counter. "So, I was going to ask your name, but I guess I have it now."

"Yes, same for you," I say to the man who balcony banged me in more than a few solo flights.

I wish I didn't feel a little spark in my chest as I look at his blue eyes, the color of the sea. Disappointment rims his gaze.

"That's me," he says, sighing heavily. "And you're you."

That's how we gave our "names" on the sidewalk the other morning. Ugh. He seems to be hating this stroke of bad luck too.

I glance around his shop. "The bike you ride makes even more sense," I continue. Wow. I'm really going to impress him with my intelligence.

"And this is your appointment," he says, on a rough swallow.

But, crap. He better not think I was stalking him or something. That would be so awful. "I swear, I had no idea you owned this shop. You, as in, the guy I was texting," I say, and that feels so uncomfortable on my tongue.

His brow knits. "I didn't think you knew. Not at all. Don't worry about that," he says, and whew. That's good.

I lift a hand and touch my earrings. "But thanks for these. Maybe they're not so lucky."

He frowns. "Why would you say that? Iris has been raving about you, and it sounds like you could be perfect for the job."

Oh. He still wants to hire me? Even though we were flirting like bunnies about to screw?

That's great, because I sure as hell need to put bills before boinking. I won't turn down a job just because I wanted to ask my potential new boss on a date. "I would love to work here," I say in my best professional tone.

"Great. Because Iris would kill me if I didn't hire you," Milo answers with a smile.

A fantastic smile. A sexy smile.

Stop, stop. He's almost your boss.

"I'd hate for you to die," I say, with forced cheer. I mean, I don't want him dead. Of course I don't. And I have to keep up a cheery, fun disposition.

I *need* a job so much more than I need a date.

"When can you start?"

He's no longer my almost boss. He's my official boss, and my crush is going on ice.

"Tomorrow if you want?" Best to begin as Miss Helpful rather than Miss Hot To Trot.

Milo smiles and it feels the slightest bit wistful. Like maybe he's wondering what might have been, too, over cake and beer.

But that doesn't matter.

What does matter is this—the guy I've been flirting with now signs my paychecks. And he can never know he's also Mister Sexy Pants.

10

NO JACK HOLES HERE

Milo

What kind of businessman would I be to pass on a new hire because I was attracted to her?

The worst.

That'd be rudely unfair.

Clearly, Veronica is right for the job.

Also, what kind of flaming asshole would I be if I said, *Hey, Miss Cute Devil Butt, I wanted to ask you out for cake and orgasms, so I can't hire you, but I'd like to test the strength of my couch with you?*

The kind of guy I refuse to be—a jack hole.

Which means, after Iris trains Veronica on Saturday, come Monday morning I'm working side by side in my shop with the woman I wanted to take home and bend over a piece of furniture.

As I spin the pedals on a new custom design, I steal a glance across the store to the flower half of Bikes and

Blooms where Veronica's tying a bow around a bouquet of white jasmine. Wearing a yellow *Blooms* apron cinched at the waist and a cute blue dress with white polka dots, she looks good enough to eat. And I am a bad, bad man for checking out my new manager while she rings up a curly-haired customer.

"You'll have to tell me what Maddie says. I think she's going to love the white jasmine," Veronica tells the woman, while I do my damnedest to listen rather than gawk. I'm the boss—eavesdropping is acceptable, but staring is not.

With a smile, the woman takes the massive bouquet from Veronica. "And to think I was going to get her red roses. Pfft. But these are hilarious. I mean, after popping out three babies, what could be better?"

That's odd. I stop my work on the bike, putting my glasses in my pocket then setting my tools down on the counter. Daisies often symbolize new beginnings, as well as innocence. I'm not sure how Veronica jumped to jasmine as the right gift for Maddie.

Oh, shit. What if Veronica's flower radar is out of whack? Did I hire her because I felt guilty for wanting her? Goddamn my faulty judgment.

The customer draws the bouquet to her nose and sniffs it. "Thanks . . . a bunch."

Veronica smiles, then waves goodbye to the woman as she leaves.

Since Zara's intensely discussing the merits of electric bikes with a hipster, I grab the chance to touch base with my new employee, and head to the flower side of the shop. I gesture to the front door, swinging shut behind the customer. "So, she got jasmine for a friend who had a kid? Instead of daisies?"

With a laugh, Veronica shakes her head. "Her friend just got her tubes tied."

I frown. "And she's giving her flowers?"

Veronica gives me a *silly boy* look. "Don't you know flowers are great for any occasion?" she asks sweetly.

Damn. She's right, and I am off my game. "Well, sure. That's the message we want to promote," I say, like *yup, that's what I meant to say.*

"And Tina wanted to bring Maddie something irreverent, to celebrate this end of an era and the start of a new one. But she couldn't find the right flowers online."

I like the sound of that. "Go on," I say.

"I suggested jasmine because they symbolize . . . *desire.*" Veronica gives a little shrug, just east of coy, just north of naughty. "So she wrote on the card: *Congrats, Maddie! You can get it on all the time now.* Cute, isn't it?"

"Very cute," I say evenly, so I don't reveal that my store manager's advice is gold, and, fuck, now I'm thinking about getting it on all the time with Veronica. Maybe I'm the one who needs daisies to restore my innocence. My mind just dropped to gutter levels. "So, how's your second day going so far?"

There. That's so boss-like, not perv-like.

"It's great," she says, but with a touch of forced cheer and I get it. The first few days in a new job can be tough.

"Let me know what I can do. If you need anything. Iris is the flower genius, but I've learned tons from her, and I'm happy to help. Honestly, the jasmine was a stroke of genius," I say, hoping to give her a boost of confidence.

She's quiet for a few seconds, but with her brow furrowed, her brain is busy. "Actually, I wanted to bring this up during the interview, but I was a little distracted," she says, looking me square in the eyes.

I was distracted too, but lingering on that moment when fate-flipped-us-the-bird isn't wise. "We can talk now," I say helpfully.

"Because, you know, Friday *was* a little awkward," she adds, then gives me a rueful smile, a concession to the weirdness of our situation.

It was beyond awkward, I want to shout. We texted about the importance of daily tongue-rolling, for fuck's sake. What's done is done though. "And here we are, working together," I say, pretending things aren't weird.

But what else is there for me to do? Nada.

"I wanted to share some of my ideas for how to market the shop," she offers. "Would you be open to hearing them?"

Hell yes. That's more than I expected from a new hire. "I'd love to," I say, but then the bell above the door dings, and a new customer comes in.

"Raincheck?" she asks.

"It's a date," I say before I think the better of it.

Don't say date again, you dipshit.

Especially since Veronica squints, clearly flustered by my faux pas. Well, better she should squint than cringe.

And on that put-my-foot-in-my-mouth note, I

sequester myself in my office with Trudy for the rest of the afternoon.

I don't get another chance to chat with her until the end of the day. Zara's finishing a tune-up, so I join Veronica as she sweeps flower clippings on the floor.

"So, about those ideas," I say, diving straight into business, just business.

She sets down the broom and dustpan, then points to the front of the store. "That cute chalkboard outside? I think we can mix it up each day with a new saying, and a reason to buy flowers, and post it on your social. You have a decent Instagram presence, but you could post more regularly. Here's my idea. You know how the Internet celebrates everything with a national day?"

"Like National Sandwich Day?"

Blinking, she straightens her shoulders like she's been caught daydreaming in class, then squeaks out: "Sandwiches?"

"Surely you've heard of them. Those delicious things where bread is a wrapper for other food," I say.

"Ah, yes. Thank you," she says, deadpan.

"And . . . National Sandwich Day is only one of my favorite days of the year. It's not yours?" I ask playfully.

"I'm not a fan of sandwiches," she says, then shrugs, all *no big deal* style.

I exaggerate shock, dropping my jaw, then rubbing my ear. "I must have heard wrong. How could anyone dislike sandwiches?"

"It happens," she says quickly, dismissing the topic. Maybe she had a bad experience with a sandwich. "But what are your other favorite days? Inquiring minds want to know." She sounds fascinated, as if she's wanted to discuss this with me for ages. Or maybe she's just super keen not to discuss sandwiches.

But my answer is National Sixty-Nine Day. Is that a day of celebration? If not, it should be. "National Pajama Day," I offer, tossing out something chaste. Or chaste-ish.

Veronica's pretty green eyes twinkle. "Then how about this? For each day, we come up with a fun new saying about why you need flowers. Like this: *It's National Wear Your PJs to Work Day. Give your boss some pansies to get a PJ pass.*"

"I like it," I say, stoked by her idea. "Can you do that tomorrow?"

She holds up a finger to make a point. "I can, but tomorrow is National Burrito Day, and that's not so flower-able. But there's no reason we can't make up national days too," she says, a little devilishly. "I mean, who's in charge of making up national days, anyway?"

"I applied for the position but didn't get it," I say.

She laughs. "Same here! But I bet we'd have been great at that job," she says.

Oh sweetheart, I bet we'd have been great at lots of jobs.

"If I were in charge of the national days," she goes on, "I'd deem tomorrow . . . National Get Out of Bed Day. And we can write: *Did you brush your teeth today and put on pants this morning? Then celebrate with some flowers.*"

"I'm glad you didn't get the National Day gig, Veron-ica. Because that's a good one. Want to use it tomorrow?"

She's vibrating with energy. "Iris left me some of the pastel chalks. I could write it up on the chalkboard now, and we'll post a pic overnight. See if it gets some traction in the early morning when people check Insta before they even roll out of bed."

Smarts and sex appeal. Dating isn't a game of Frogger. It's Russian Roulette.

"That sounds perfect," I say.

Grabbing the chalk and an eraser, she pops outside and tackles her project. When she's done, she snaps a pic as the sun sets behind her.

She comes back in and stands next to me, showing me the shot on her phone. It's a good picture, but I catch the scent of her hair, and I should definitely study the picture longer since I'm dying to know what that fragrance is . . .

Picking out scents in this shop calls for the nose of a sommelier, but I've got one, and pretty sure that's not Bikes and Blooms flowers that I'm smelling.

It's . . . orange blossom.

Just a faint trace of it from Veronica's hair. Or maybe on her neck. Or her skin.

Stop!

I clear my throat, inch away from the tempting scent. "Great shot. Want to send it to me and I can post it?"

"I can do it now if you want. I mean, I'm not *that* dangerous on the Internet," she says, and the corner of her lips twitch. There's a hidden meaning there, but I'm busy trying to erase orange blossom from my memory bank.

After she sends me the pic, I give her my phone for posting but stay next to her. I learned a lesson or two from Callie, and I'm not about to hand over the keys to the social kingdom to just anyone yet.

"And tomorrow there'll be a line around the block," she says as she hands me back my phone.

"I'll hold you to that," I say.

A few minutes later, she leaves, then Zara takes off after her.

Whew. I lock the door once more, then I get as far away from the flowers as I can, working on a custom design for a while, letting bike grease fill my nostrils until I can't smell oranges anymore.

I work until my phone pings at eight, reminding me I'm meeting my brother for a beer. After I take off my glasses, I wash up, and Trudy and I head out into the warm June night.

When I spot Bryan at an outside table at The Lucky Spot, he waggles a bottle my way. "I ordered for you. Figured you'd want to reward yourself for making it through your first few days. You better have been on good behavior," he says, since he knows the story. I caught him up to speed when we went for a ride on the High Line over the weekend.

I take the cold beer and tip the neck to his. "Today was National I Was a Good Boy Day."

He gives me a curious look, then makes a rolling gesture with his hand. I give him the deets on Veronica's National Day plan.

Laughing, he shakes his head. "Good luck, buddy.

She sounds sharp, and I already know you like her yoga pants."

I hang my head. "Too fucking much."

"I guess every day at work now will be Good Boy Day," he says.

"Every. Single. Day."

On that note, I take a pull of my beer and buckle in. It's going to be a long, hot summer.

After we grab some grub, and chat about Bryan's new business plans, we say goodnight and go our separate ways.

When I reach my block, I'm determined to keep my eyes on the sidewalk the entire way to my building, my focus on my dog, not my neighbor's building. I do not look up just in case Veronica's standing on her balcony again.

Jesus, man. This isn't Romeo and Juliet.

I don't even like Shakespeare. I mean, I get that he's a wordsmith and all, but in high school, I could not for the life of me figure out all those *thou, thines,* and *thys.* Science and fixing things were more my speed and still are.

But now that I'm near her building, I find myself glancing up in spite of myself. One look won't hurt, will it? Nope.

This isn't my high school Shakespeare at all.

It's more like Naughty Juliet, since Veronica's standing by the balcony, eyes closed, a low-cut tank top hugging her breasts. She's talking into her phone, leaning against the railing and . . . hold on. Are those sleep shorts?

Is it National Pajama Night and no one told me?

Licking my lips, I try to look away, but her mouth is moving, and I swear for a few seconds, I can make out the shape of words.

Words like *tell me what you want.*

No idea what she's saying, but she goes through some kind of list. One, two, three, four, five.

Then, Trudy jerks her gaze to a nearby tree and barks at a scampering squirrel.

Veronica's eyes fly open and meet mine.

Busted.

11

SURVIVAL TIPS

Veronica

I'm on my balcony, lounging in sleep shorts and a tank, cooling myself off with a handheld pink fan since it's boob hot. The kind of hot where I already yanked off that titty prison of a bra, twirled it around on my finger and tossed it on the bed an hour ago.

It's Monday night, I taught a Little Artists class after work, and now I've got a panting dog curled up by my thigh, my laptop on my lap, and a mojito in my hand. I'm as prepared as I'll ever be to answer questions online at The Dating Pool.

Mild-mannered florist by day . . . sexpert by night.

Though maybe I should amend that to mild-mannered florist by day who pretends to hate sandwiches so her boss won't figure out she's the fuck-me-and-feed-me-paninis anonymous sex columnist.

What a smooth save that was.

Not.

Milo seems cool and all, but you never know when someone will flip out. Agnes is a case in point. The last thing I need is to lose a solid temporary job. I suspect it's an unwritten rule that writing about banging your boss is grounds for firing.

On that note, I need a drink. Twirling my metal straw in the glass, I take a fueling gulp of the cocktail, then set it beside my chair on the balcony. I stroke Stud-Muffin's head. "I've got this. I'm going to earn some coffee change and talk about sex without thinking about anyone in particular," I tell my Chihuahua boy.

He lifts his chin, asking for a scratch.

I comply, focusing on the dog. Not the man who stood so close to me when I was posting the chalkboard picture on Instagram.

I click over to The Dating Pool and get cracking, starting with this question from SingleInTheCity21.

How do you know if you're going to like a fantasy? I have all these wild ones that I'm afraid to try since—what if reality just doesn't live up? And then, what if I spend all my time in my fantasies and I never try the real thing?

Whew. That's a lot, but I dive in to unpack her concerns one by one.

Dear SingleInTheCity21,

I hear ya! I worry about the same things. What if the real thing doesn't compare? What if I can't get out of my head when I finally get down to business?
But even if you're having a party of one, why not make that the best it can be? If that's a quickie, and all you need is a zero-to-sixty toy, then go for that. If you want to indulge in a long, slow, delicious fantasy involving role-play, and dirty talk, and blindfolds (ahem, sounds fun to me!), then go for that. As for whether reality lives up—your party of one is reality too. Enjoy it fully. If fantasy is better than reality, I say make the most of your fantasies!

Xoxo

Your Friendly Neighborhood Virgin

I hit post, then click to other questions, where I find a common theme.

Fantasies.

Seems Bellamy was onto something.

I close the laptop, set it on the balcony, then put my pooch down too, so I can stand and take my phone from my pocket.

Moving to the railing, I hit record, closing my eyes as the words form.

I Had a Dream About You . . .

Show of hands. Ever had a dirty dream about someone and then seen them the next day?

Oh, sure. It's just me.

C'mon, we've all done it. In the light of day, you feel a little shy, a little transparent. Wondering things like . . . Can everyone tell that Bob O'Malley from accounting ate me out on the copier last night in my sleep? Or maybe you're all pink in the cheeks because Daryl Mayberry in legal did a striptease for you in the break room to "I Dreamed a Dream," and you still shouted for him to take it all off even though Fantine was dying.

You woke up embarrassed, maybe even confused, but definitely turned on.

Look, I'm still raising my hand. (And yes, those are dreams I dreamed once upon a time, though names have been changed to protect the innocent.)

Those dreams made me wonder what I craved. But my daydreams and my bedtime fantasies drive me to think about my wishes and wants too.

I want a guy to say to me . . . *tell me what you want.*

And I'll tell him. Because I've got a list, starting with my top-five fantasies.

1. Speak up. If we're kissing all hot and heavy, and you're making these rough, growly noises, I'll know

how much you're enjoying yourself. Give me sounds, murmurs, and sweet, dirty words, please.

2. Make me laugh. Sex is funny if you think about it, from the positions to the squeaks to the sheer mechanics. If you can make me laugh during sex, I bet the nookie will be better.

3. Spank me, pull my hair, push me down. I'm not a doll, so don't treat me like one. I'm a grown woman. I won't break. Bite me, hard, there, right there.

4. Be in the shower one night when I get home. Let me find you by following the sound of pattering water. I'll walk in on you. Only, you're not getting clean. You're getting dirty . . . and I'm getting wet.

5. Tell me you thought about me all day, and I'm yours.

So, dear reader, I encourage you to make your own list. Write down your dirty dreams, and then decide if you want to find out how much you like sex on a copy machine.

Or not.

For now, I have a date with my Just for Her Diamond Flicker, and I'm going to pick something from my top-five menu.

***

Before I can sign off, a high-pitched bark rips through the air.

My eyes pop open and find StudMuffin, sniffing sage in a pot on the deck. But I know he didn't bark—the sound came from below. I peer over the railing, and my breath catches when I find the culprit.

That's my boss on the sidewalk, and his dog is barking at me.

Think fast.

I hit end on the recording, so I don't lose my work, then I wrack my brain.

What do I do now?

Act innocent. It's the best defense. Besides, did he even hear me?

Time to find out.

"Hi, there," I say at the same volume as I dictated my column. "I was recording some thoughts on my favorite flowers and whether every day should be National Pizza Day. Yup, just working late on brilliant ideas."

Totally not dictating a sex column.

Milo shakes his head and cups his ear, the universal sign for *I can't hear you.*

Thank goddess!

Trudy tugs insistently on her leash. He points to her and then waves, and when he walks into his building next door, I do believe I've been saved by a dog.

Whew. That was close. I go inside and clean up the

dinner dishes, both because I need to and because I need a distraction to get Milo out of my head.

My column won't do a damn thing to get his hotness off my mind.

When the sink is spick-and-span, I dry my hands, then head to the kitchen table to clean up my transcription. Before I can start, my phone pings.

Oh!

It's Milo texting. I click on his note as I head into my bedroom to read it.

Milo: Hey! Sorry if Trudy scared you. We'd just come home from drinks with my brother, and she must have spotted you on your balcony and wanted to say hi.

Aww, his dog likes me.

Veronica: Your dog has excellent taste.

Milo: Yes, she does. Anyway, didn't want to worry you.

Why would he think I was worried? He couldn't hear my top-five list.

I text back as I flop onto my bed.

Veronica: It's all good. She didn't freak me out. I hope you had a nice time with your brother.

There. That's not flirty at all. We're simply having a nice, civilized, professional-ish conversation.

Milo: I wouldn't call it nice. More like very intense trash talk and one-upmanship. But hey, that's what brothers do.

That's sweet, Milo telling me about his family.

Veronica: Older or younger? Wait. Let me guess. He's older and he's always telling you what to do, but he's the first one at the door ready to pick you up when you're down?

Milo: Let me guess. You have one of your own.

I settle into my purple, red, and orange pillows as I clutch the device and reply.

Veronica: I have one of those in the form of a sister. They have so many ideas, older siblings.

Milo: And they always know best.

Veronica: And they aren't afraid to tell you.

Milo: But truth be told, I think he is. I'm going to miss him when he moves to LA.

Someone is chatty. Milo doesn't seem to want to let this convo go any more than I do. It's nine-thirty at night, but that's not terribly late, so I reply with a question.

Veronica: Why is he moving?

Milo: Bryan's a contractor. He specializes in makeovers and restoring homes, and he has a big opportunity in LA. Can you believe he's leaving me for a job? Sheesh!

Veronica: The nerve!

Milo: My thoughts exactly. There should be a sibling law against that. Anyway, he'll take off later this summer. For now, I try to see him as much as possible, which means I get my supply of brotherly advice on the reg. Is your sister in New York?

I shouldn't read anything into this—how long we've been texting, how casually personal this feels, how quickly he's replying. People can enjoy texting other people without it meaning they're going to have sex on the copy machine the next day.

Veronica: Yes, she's in the city. She's a romance writer. And my biggest cheerleader and a total pain in the butt, and if she ever tried to move, I would lock her in my cupboard and make her stay.

Milo: LOL! (Also, I don't usually write LOL, but if we were in person I'd laugh, so it only seems fair to let you know you made me laugh.)

I tense, eyeing the phone like it's spying on me. *Make me laugh* was an item on my top-five fantasies list. Fine, *make me laugh* is a broad command, but is this some subtle way of telling me he heard me? But there's no way to ask without sounding paranoid. Instead, I stick to the light-hearted mood.

Veronica: On behalf of the Fairness in Texting Council, I humbly accept your reasoning.

Milo: Do you ever want to write, like your sister? Since you worked in publishing, I was just curious.

. . .

Ugh. My shoulders sink. I don't want him to connect the dots between me and my secret writing identity. I hate this, but I have no choice.

Veronica: I think all the romance writing genes went to her.

But after I hit send, I feel like a dirty little liar. Maybe I can be *direct-ish* about other topics.

Veronica: By the way, I was dictating my to-do list when Trudy said hello. Tell her I say hi too.

That's honest enough, but it protects my anonymity with my column.

Milo: She sends her regards to StudMuffin and you as well. Also, thanks for reminding me of my failures in life. My New Year's resolution was to do a better job at keeping a to-do list, but then I forgot to write it down.

I can't even laugh at the joke. Is he serious? Can anyone be?

Veronica: I AM SHOOK. You don't keep a list? How do you function?

Milo: I try to remember everything.

Veronica: Good luck with that. Sidenote: I love lists. Adore them. I want to date lists. We'll have to do a National List Day.

Milo: Sounds like a wild date. Sidenote: Can 'order flowers for everyone' be on the work list?

Veronica: Obviously.

Milo: Anyway, I don't want to commandeer all your time. I need to go write a list. I hope you had a good evening, Veronica.

I stare at his name a little longer, a little wistfully. But it's for the best that he's shutting down our conversation, even though I love the way he used my name, and I don't even know why.

Except, it feels deliciously personal. And not the least bit professional.

Veronica: See you tomorrow, Milo.

Milo: Night, Glitter Gal.

And that feels even more personal, his nickname for me. I set a hand to my suddenly racing heart, then put my phone down, before the exchange veers even further away from professional.

I head to the kitchen table, clean up the transcription of my column on my laptop, then send it to Bellamy before I call it a night.

When I slide into bed a little later, I click back to the texts. I can't resist re-reading the messages as I settle under the sheets. They send a tingle down my spine. So much that when I put down my phone for good, it's not the last device I use before I fall asleep.

But even if Milo entered my fantasies, at least I kept Mister Sexy Pants out of my column. That's a solid step in my program of de-crush-ification.

In the morning, I'm at the bathroom mirror, slicking on Two Pink Lips gloss while Hot Stuff sniffs my hair. This cat loves my shampoo. When he tries to rub his head against my blow-dried locks, I inch away. He gives me the stink eye, then resorts to watching my every move from his perch on the vanity when my phone beeps.

I get a burst of excitement at the thought that it could be Milo, wanting to walk with me to work. I'd say yes in a heartbeat, but the message isn't from him.

It's Bellamy, and I try not to be disappointed.

Being the badass boss lady she is, she's already read my column. *I love literally everything about this installment . . . but can you pretty please add Mister Sexy Pants to it? Like maybe in between the fictional Bob O'Malley and Daryl Mayberry? The readers love Mister Sexy Pants. He's become something of a legend here at The Dating Pool.*

I groan. More like a legend in my own mind.

But I reply with, *Of course.* While I'm tapping out the message with the phone on the counter, Hot Stuff stretches then saunters across my phone, stepping on the screen with his gigantic paws. "Dude," I chide, but he's already leaped to the floor and is off to the living room to likely lick something.

Not his balls though.

I glance back at the phone screen, figuring he fired off another note prematurely. But the email he walked on is safe and sound in drafts. "Seriously?" I grumble. "You couldn't have sent *that* email? You had to send the one to Agnes?"

I catch a final glimpse of the big boy before he slinks into the kitchen. He holds his head high, and he is definitely giving me the butt.

I sigh and add a line for Bellamy at the end of the column. That seems the better place for Mister Sexy Pants. Then I send her the edited closing paragraph:

For now, I'm going to grab my Just for Her Diamond Flicker because I have a dream date with Mister Sexy Pants and my imagination.

.   .   .

Well, it's the truth.

I hit send, finish my primping, and as I drop my gloss into my purse, I get a new message in my inbox—from Blanche.

Huh. I didn't think I'd hear from her again so soon.

Dear Veronica,

I can't thank you enough. Your recommendation was spot on. Pun intended. In any case, do not hesitate to reach out when you're ready to look for work again. I will do my best to help you.

Blanche

I'm pretty sure her offer is a tit for tat, but that works for me. I'll definitely cash in the favor soon enough. I shoot her a quick reply, telling her about my new job and thanking her for checking in, then head to the kitchen, where I grab a pen and check the calendar of firemen and rescue pets that Ellie gave me for Christmas.

Six weeks from now, I'll begin my redemption job search with the hope of snagging a new publishing gig by the end of the summer. Hazel said she'll be talking to her editor soon, feeling out Lancaster Abel Books about possible openings on the children's side. She's asking her writer friend TJ, as well, to keep his ear to the ground.

I circle the date and write *blastoff* in the square. Then I grab my purse, kiss my pets goodbye on their wet noses, and head to work.

When I arrive fifteen minutes later, Milo's back is to me, and he's bent over a bike on a stand, giving me a perfect view of his ass, all firm and muscular in a pair of snug jeans that are unfairly sexy.

Why am I so into his booty?

No idea, but I want to grab his ass. Preferably while he's deep inside me.

I manage to tear my gaze off his rear, but oops, it lands on his strong, toned, inked arms, which move fluidly as he builds a mint-green custom bike. He's wearing a tank top today, giving me a full view of his tattoo for the first time. It's so unusual. Is it hydrogen molecules? The chemical composition for oxygen maybe?

"What's your tattoo for?" I blurt, even though it gives away that I've been staring. "The one on your right arm?"

From behind his glasses, his blue gaze drifts to his ink, then he turns to me, a smile spreading slowly. "I studied chemistry in college. I'm kind of a geek." He holds out his arms, almost like he's inviting me to touch. *I wish.* "It's the chemical composition for body hormones."

I sway, grabbing hold of the wall next to me. God help me.

"You okay?" he asks.

"I'm great," I squeak, as a flush sweeps over my neck.

"You look a little hot. I think it's going to be in the eighties today . . ."

"Yeah, feels like five hundred," I mutter, turning away from him.

If he looks me in my eyes, he'll know I had a dirty dream about him last night.

Only it was more than a dream. Dreams come in the middle of the night.

Fantasies help us to come before we sleep.

I make a hard right and head straight for the display case for the flowers where I yank open the door to cool off.

12

BOOBS ON THE HALF SHELL

Milo

All of Tuesday, I berate myself for my text transgression the night before.

Though technically, I made several text transgressions. Using her nickname, texting so late, and acting like the whole damn convo was a Lay's potato chip—couldn't eat just one.

But I have to stop snacking on Veronica's texts. What's it going to lead to?

Dognapping. Bike stealing. Tanking my business with bad reviews.

So I course correct, talking politely to all my employees, like Zara and my part-time mechanic James, as well as Veronica, asking how they're doing, and zipping my lips when it comes to flirty comments.

I spend most of the day in the back of the store, working on a handmade hybrid for a customer who wants to commute across the Brooklyn Bridge each day to the office.

When I hop on my bike after work for an evening ride, I renew my vows.

Like a devoted monk, I abstain from late-night texting on Tuesday night, and all through the next day too, giving my full attention to the store so I can claw my way out of the five thousand dollar hole.

I've seen a slight uptick in flower sales thanks to Veronica's National Day efforts, so that's another reason to lay off the Lay's.

On Thursday night, Zara takes off early, and James signs out too, leaving Veronica and me to close. At six twenty-five, I'm finishing adding new reflecting pedals to a bike as Trudy noses a stuffed alligator toy in the corner of the shop.

Veronica's busy helping a good-looking, forty-something guy in a tailored suit pick out flowers. "I bet these would do the trick," she says, guiding him to a bucket of orange roses. Then her lips turn up in a devilish grin. "You could add coral too. Those will get your message across even more."

The silver fox hums for a few seconds then nods. "I should probably do both then."

"Go for doubles, I like to say."

I whimper silently. I want doubles with her. Hell, singles would do.

"You're brilliant . . . Veronica," the man says, and out of the corner of my eye I catch him reading her name tag.

Hold on.

Is the dude flirting with her while he's buying flowers for his lover? I rise, adjusting the bike seat as I listen in.

"Why, thank you," Veronica says. "Let me just put these bouquets together. Two dozen of each, right?"

"Yes. I was going to just get a dozen, but this seems to send a better message . . ."

"It sure does," she says, as she arranges the flowers. "Anything else planned for your special night? Dinner out, dinner in?"

The customer smirks.

It's the kind of look a man gives when he plans a seductive evening for his woman. "*In*. Definitely in. And while we're at it, I hope you don't mind my asking, but I want to give her a little something sexy to wear too." His voice dips like he's the slightest bit shy, but not shy enough to stop. But I take the question to mean the dude's not hitting on her, and that's a damn good thing.

"Any suggestions on where I could go at this hour? I'm a little late."

She ties a piece of twine into a bow, as she answers, "Try You Look Pretty Today. They opened a second shop here in the Village. It's a great lingerie store and the owner is so helpful."

"Great," he says. "Appreciate that."

And I appreciate Veronica's upsell to four-dozen flowers, but why did the dude have to mention unmentionables? Now I'm thinking of teddys, nighties, and those cropped bras that can fry a man's brain.

I bet Veronica wears one of those bras. Boobs on the half shell I call them.

Yup, in one fell swoop, there goes my monkish restraint. Here comes my curious cat. Once the customer leaves, I flip the sign on the door to say *closed*, then make my way to Veronica's half of the shop.

"So now customers are asking for lingerie recommendations? I'm a little surprised," I say, editing out the part where I ask: *how do you know so much about what people need, from friendship to the boudoir?* Her expertise is unexpected. "No shade on Iris—my friend does a great job—but no one ever asked her where to get underwear."

Veronica laughs softly then drops her voice to a conspiratorial whisper. "No one is getting anyone underwear, Milo. He's getting his wife of twenty years a teddy, a garter belt, and stockings."

I blink, a little hot under the collar. "He told you that?"

"He might as well have. It's a Thursday night and he's bringing her flowers that represent passion. I think it's safe to say he's not popping into the nearest Target to grab her the store brand three-pack of cotton undies on sale for half off," she says, as she organizes the display of greeting cards on the counter.

But I bet you'd look good enough to eat in the Target brand, or any brand, or nothing at all.

"Good for them," I say, but it comes out strangled. I try again to get to the heart of the matter. "I've gotta say —customers like talking to you. You're like an Ask Me Anything of the flower world."

As she stacks the cards, she gives a little shrug. "It's probably because of my freckles." She wiggles her nose, showing off the spray of dots across her nose. "Supposedly, they make me seem more approachable and less threatening. Who knew freckles were so . . . inviting? But mostly, I give off an ask-me-anything vibe. I probably should have worked at an information desk. Maybe I missed my true calling."

In her corner, Trudy chomps down on the toy gator.

The soundtrack of a dog killing a stuffy puts us in safer territory than lingerie chatter. "You have a gift, Veronica, and I'm glad this worked out. I needed someone who could take the bloom side of the business under her wing. I've had a lot to deal with since Trudy came back."

She tilts her head. "Where was she?"

Ah, shit. I didn't intend to go there, but I walked into that. "With my ex," I say, the words as bitter as the memory of Callie's lying, stealing, and cheating. "We had a dog custody thing. She took Trudy, even though she was mine. I adopted her years before I even met my ex, but I had to go to arbitration to get her back, and . . ." I stop myself before I go further. No one likes hearing about past loves, especially from their boss. "And now she's mine again."

Veronica winces. "That sounds terrible." She crosses the shop, stopping at Trudy, whose mouth is full of green fur. "Sweet girl, are you glad to be home?" she asks.

Trudy drops the toy and licks Veronica's hand.

Fuck me, that is too sweet. I better not look, or my heart will scamper over to the two of them.

But I can't pull my gaze away from the sight of the woman petting my dog.

"Yes, you are, you sweetie-pie. You're back with your person."

Be still, my beating heart. Veronica didn't say *baby* to the dog, or *dog daddy* to me, and I couldn't be happier.

Veronica stands and smooths out her apron. "She's clearly yours, and I'm glad she's back."

"Me too," I say, and since some truths bear repeating, I say it again. "Me too." Then I shift gears, moving away from this getting-to-know-you chat. It could lead to text transgressions later. "Anyway, we're both glad you're here."

"Thank you," Veronica says, and lets out a long breath as she returns to closing up, grabbing the broom to sweep. "I really like the job so far, and I need it," she says as I join her, sorting the flowers in the cooler case.

"But you do want to return to publishing," I say. This job is temporary. It ends in three months.

"Definitely, but I'm glad to do this in the meantime." Her voice is a little tight.

I want to ask what happened at her last gig, but chances are her company let her go because of cutbacks or some stupid shit. A part of me imagines asking her out in three months when we're no longer working together. But entertaining that line of thinking won't get me through the rest of the summer, so I table those dangerous thoughts.

"Do you think you'll return to editing? Or is there a list-making side of the publishing business you could go to?" I ask with a smile.

She smiles back. "Editing definitely. Making lists is about the extent of my writing skills."

I arch a dubious brow. "I have to disagree. I think you're selling yourself short. Your sister might have the romance-writing genes, but your chalkboard posts are pretty clever."

Snorting, she waves a hand. "That's just social media stuff. Besides, I love editing. I was a total bookworm as a kid."

"The kind who brought a flashlight under the covers to read well past midnight?"

With softness in her gaze, she nods. "I had reading forts everywhere. We grew up in Wistful, Connecticut, and Hazel and I even tried to convince our dad to build us a tree house for reading."

"And did he?"

Her fond expression vanishes. "He said once we mastered the four forms of the conditional tense, we could have a tree house."

"Ouch. Sounds like a tough guy," I say, but I suspect that's an understatement.

"And he wonders why his marriage didn't work out," she says heavily, jaw tight. I could tell her my dad's a prick too, but when Veronica resumes sweeping, she steers the conversation back to lighter grounds. "And were you under the covers with beakers and Bunsen burners?"

I laugh. "Full geek, Veronica. *But,* I did all the seed-in-a-jar and soil-testing experiments known to middle school."

"Ah, the blooms part of Bikes and Blooms started early. And now you're selling orange and coral roses to men who adore their wives and buy them lingerie." Those green eyes twinkle again as they meet mine. "What if tomorrow is National Lingerie Day?"

Here we go again.

What if tomorrow is National This Will Be the Death of My Restraint Day?

I swallow past the desert in my throat. "Yeah, that sounds great," I rasp out, closing the cooler door.

"What's better for a Friday night? A romantic evening and a passionate night in," she says.

"Nothing," I say in a smoky voice that's just shy of betraying my desire.

"Then let's make it so."

"By the power vested in you by the National Day Council, tomorrow is . . . Lingerie Day," I say, like a declaration.

We set up the chalkboard outside and she writes the new tagline, then takes the photo. Back inside, she sends the pic to me, and I upload it in a draft.

"Do you want to write a caption? The others you did were pretty catchy," I say. She's shown she's got a magic touch with words.

"What if we do something that makes it seem like we're telling a story about a Friday night?"

"What do you mean exactly?" I ask, enrapt. She might be casting a spell on me already.

"Something about . . ." She glances over the bikes, but she seems faraway in her thoughts. "*Friday is my favorite night of the week. Bring me flowers and when you come home, I'll be wearing a little lace, listening to an undress-me tunes playlist. Make your Friday night the kind of night worth waiting all week for."*

When she turns back to me, her eyes have a dreamy look in them. I couldn't see them on Monday night when she was on her balcony, but I know, without a doubt, that's how she looked on her balcony.

She's got this sensual energy about her. I can feel it wafting off her. It feels the same as when she talked into her phone into the summer night.

She's Naughty Juliet.

And I am Too Hard Romeo.

"That's really good," I say thickly, my brain a storm of erotic images. "Sounds like a great Friday."

"Mmm. It sure does," she says, perhaps still a little lost in the haze as she takes my phone and types. My resolve crumbles a little more when I catch another whiff of her. "Is that . . . orange blossom?" I whisper.

She raises her face, those big eyes glimmering. "You have a very good nose, Milo."

I would love to use it to learn all the flavors of her skin. But I have to resist.

I clear my throat, the sound a dividing line between my flirty alter ego and my reluctant monk. "I'm going to, um, finish that bike," I say roughly, hoping my voice doesn't give away where my body is at, and that my words don't reveal the lie. I'm done with the bike.

But I fiddle with it, hoping it'll take my mind off Veronica as she finishes closing up. When she's done, I could make an excuse to stay, but I find myself leaving with her, and my dog.

After all, there's nothing flirty about walking. It's a practical activity involving placing one foot after the other.

Out on the street, I take one last glance at the sign advertising National Lingerie Day. I try to fight off the urge to talk about lingerie.

But I'm woefully unsuccessful. I've got underthings on my mind. "So, undies don't cut it? Do we say lacy numbers? Sexy panties? And while we're at it, what about bra? It sounds so practical, but then, those half-bra thingamajigs hardly seem practical."

She giggles. "Do you mean a demi-cup bra?"

I snap my fingers with my free hand. "Yes, that's it. I forgot what it was called."

"Demi cups are sexy. But, no, not at all practical," she says.

"Shame, that," I say, my mind drifting off as Trudy trots in front of us.

"And when you're peddling flowers and passion and romance, then underthings should be lacy lingerie, and so on," Veronica says, then slings her purse higher on her shoulder. The move dislodges the strap of her dress. It falls down her arm, nestling in the crook of her elbow.

That strap. That lucky piece of strap. I look away. If I find out she's wearing a demi cup, I will melt into a puddle of *once upon a man.*

I point to my favorite girl, prancing along. "You know, you can bring StudMuffin to work if you want. I have a shop dog. We could probably manage two shop dogs."

She sets a hand on her heart. "Aw, I wish. You've met him. They love him at doggy daycare, but he's kind of a dick with strangers and bikes. And your girl is such a sweetheart."

I laugh. "Trudy's a good one."

"How did you wind up with that name? Trudy's unusual and I've been curious since that day I met you on the street."

I smile, picturing my dog's namesake. "My grandma —Mom's mom—was close with my brother and me. Helped raise us. Her name was Gertrude, and she loved dogs. She asked me to name a dog after her one day. So I did."

Veronica sighs happily. "That's really lovely, Milo."

My heart squeezes at the thought of my grandma. "She had a good, long life. A healthy one. I hope Trudy will have the same. Now, it's your turn. Where does StudMuffin come from?"

Veronica dips her face as we reach the street corner. I nudge her side with my elbow. "C'mon, 'fess up."

"You've seen him. He's a sexy beast," she says, with a little smoke and fire in her voice. "And so is my cat."

"Is his name Casanova?" I ask.

She shakes her head. "Nope. Hot Stuff."

"So, pretty much the same," I say.

"Yup. I guess I just like romance, and well..."

I fill in the *and well*.

Sex.

She likes sex and romance and talking about it and helping others find more of it in their lives.

From the names of her pets to the names of her lipstick, from the devils on her butt to her knowledge of lingerie, Veronica Valentine is a woman who's in touch with her sexy side.

So much for my attempts to clear my mind. Guess I won't be joining a monastery after all.

13

____

MISTER SEXY PANTS

Milo

Summer is a busy season for bikes, so the store is buzzing most days with customers. The whole crew pitches in, with Zara and James on the bike side, and another part-timer named Ian, a local community college student, as our swing. He helps out where needed, with Ian handling both pedals for bikes and petals for flowers.

One week turns into the next, turns into the next. On a sunny midweek morning, I wear trim, plaid pants to work, and Zara cracks up. "Are you trying to bring retro duds back into fashion?"

"Trying to? I believe I already did," I say.

Zara rolls her eyes, cracking up. "Veronica," Zara says, shouting across the store. "Have you heard? Our boss is a trendsetter with his fashion-plate pants."

The employer in me likes that Zara's included

Veronica in the camaraderie, but the man really wants to hear what the florist has to say about my clothes.

Veronica glances up from the tulips she's setting in the display case. "Pants are the worst," she says, a little impishly.

Huh.

That's not quite an answer. But I lose interest in pants as my gaze lingers on her skirt.

She does wear skirts all the time.

Every single day.

God bless her.

The day she flashed me her panties, she had on a red, polka-dotted one.

"Maybe tomorrow should be National Skirt Day. Maybe even Red Polka Dot Skirt Day," I add with a wink, just for her.

Veronica's eyes flicker with surprise, then with a heat that I feel all the way across the store.

* * *

The National Day themes lure more customers and bring new online reviews. But each time one pops up, I tense, dreading that it could be one of Callie's awful exes trying to trash me again. I did everything I could to bury those nasty comments, but now and then, they resurface.

But so far, so good.

They're short and sweet, like, *Bikes and Blooms will find the flower pairings you never knew you needed*, and, *Go for the flowers, stay for the recommendations!*

On a Saturday evening, nearly five weeks after Veronica started working at the shop, I'm in my office, emailing a supplier, when my phone pings, signaling another new review.

I click on the alert, bracing myself for a slap in the face.

But I relax once more as I read: *Love the new florist! She knows how to find the right blooms for any occasion! And she sure knows her other gifties too. Love her recs. She deserves all the buzz!*

Huh.

That's quite a review, and quite intriguing. Maybe this person means the lingerie recommendation? But *gifties* is ringing a naughtier bell.

I swear I've heard Iris use that word. I plug *gifties* into Google, then add *sexy* for fun.

And it's a damn good thing I'm using an incognito browser. The third search result is the sex toy brand Just for Her. The slogan promises a vibrator is *the giftie that keeps on giving.*

Oh, hell yes.

That would probably bring us repeat business. I switch to my phone, calling up the review there.

Then, I take a beat to devise a plan. It's not like I can say, *Are you recommending sex toys on the sly? If so, that is fuck hot.*

But I can drop clues. Test her reaction.

Phone in hand, I head for Veronica.

When she finishes ringing up two dozen lilacs for a salt-and-pepper-haired lady, my new florist turns to me, eyes sparkling. "Confession: lilacs are my favorite flowers," she says. "I always get excited when customers want them."

Confession: I'm excited now, thinking how Veronica would smell if I locked the door, tucked a lilac behind her ear, then leaned in to inhale her.

And kissed her all over, then asked what toy she likes best.

But I strike that sensual fantasy from my head. "Check this out." I turn the phone to show her the praise, then keep my tone light as I skirt the topic. "Maybe you do want to confess. Are you running an underground gift advice business here at the shop?"

Her eyes widen with a flicker of fear, but the look passes quickly as she gives a casual shrug and a smile.

"You've figured out my secret," she says, all playful.

Damn. I'm more confused, but I've got to know. It's just too tasty a treat for me to walk away from.

I park an elbow on the counter. "Yup. I knew it. You're an anonymous expert at . . ."

I don't say *gifties*. I want her to connect the dots. But at the word *anonymous* she swallows, looks away. Only, when she returns her gaze to me, her smile has turned devilish. "At flower recommendations, of course."

Nice sidestep, but I'm not quite buying it. *Think, Milo, think.*

I mean, if she's a secret agent for Just for Her, imagine the buzz—all puns aside—she'd generate for the store.

I can't resist. "You do give amazing flowers recs, that's for sure. But you're good at gift suggestions in general. Is that a special skill of yours?"

C'mon. Just admit it. Say you're an agent for good—the good of orgasms.

But her expression doesn't change at all. "Thanks, I try. And sometimes customers ask me for recommendations for lingerie, as you know, and restaurants and stuff," Veronica says, breezily. "PJs too. Thanks to all the National Days."

Then, the door swings open and a new customer comes in. I walk away, wondering what *stuff* is.

But I bet it involves gifties.

I know you have a secret, Miss Cute Devil Butt.

* * *

On Sunday afternoon, I put secrets and stuff far out of my head while I chill with my friends at the arcade.

I cock my arm, then roll the heavy ball up the lane.

The Skee-Ball jumps in the air, dancing close to the thirty-point hole, then it lands and sinks. "Yes! I am the stud of Skee-Ball," I declare, showboating in front of my friends Axel and Drew, and my brother. We're at Let the Good Times Roll in Chelsea.

"Not so fast," a familiar voice deadpans from my side.

Shit, I forgot Drew didn't take his final turn in the game. He's at the lane next to mine. No way will I beat him with my arm. Maybe my mind, though. I like to win at Skee-Ball, a tall order against an NFL quarterback, but maybe I can trip him up on a technicality. "Don't you have a clause or something in your contract that says you can't play games like this?"

Flashing a confident grin, Drew reaches for a ball. "That's for dangerous shit, like ziplining and parachuting. But Skee-Ball? I'm sure it can only improve my excellent arm." Then he sends the orb right at one of the toughest targets and adds one hundred points to his score. "Yes!" he shouts.

My brother pats my shoulder sympathetically. "Some guys have to show off," he says.

Drew goes down the line, pointing at each of us. "I make you all play harder when you try to beat me. Now pay up."

He rubs his fingers together. I grab some bills from my wallet and slap them in his palm. Axel does too, and Bryan follows suit. Once Drew's collected his bet, we leave the games behind and grab a table at the bar and order a round.

I haven't seen the whole crew like this in a few months—Axel was traveling in Europe, researching his latest novel, and Drew lives in California, but he spends time in New York during the summers.

It's good to see the guys again. When I was with Callie, I didn't spend much time with my friends. She didn't like it when I hung out with anyone but her.

Man, I wish I'd read the warning signs sooner.

But then, when I was a kid, I didn't see the signs that my dad was cheating on my mom. Maybe my douche-radar has been on the fritz my whole life, and I'm destined to misread people.

Hell, I'm not terribly good at figuring out Veronica either.

I suppose it's safer with her on the platonic side,

even though my dick disagrees. But he and I don't often see eye to eye.

When the server brings us beers, I thank her then offer a toast. "To . . . adulting," I say, more heavily than I expect.

Axel knits his brow. "You're no fun."

"Tell me about it," I say.

My brother clinks his bottle to mine. "I take it your half-hearted toast has something to do with your Be a Good Boy project?"

Drew sits up taller. "I want to hear about this. Are you behaving, Milo?"

"Yes, and I have no idea if this is good or bad. But I know this much—it's both character-building and dick-torturing, having to work with someone you're wickedly attracted to," I mutter.

Bryan laughs humorlessly. "I'll drink to that." One of his ex-boyfriends is a carpenter he worked with, and the results from that dating decision were disastrous.

"Another reason why I work alone," Axel says, a little smug.

Drew leans forward, meeting my gaze. "What's the story? I miss hearing your romantic woes. They make me feel better about myself."

"Gee thanks," I say, drily. But I do want to talk about Veronica. Working with her all day winds up my libido. Trying to understand her tangles my brain. But lately, I feel more than lust. Whether I can figure out her secret or not, I can't stop thinking about her. She's funny, clever, bright, and seems to have a fascinating life outside of work. The more I get to know her, the more I want to know her.

"So there's this woman who took over for Iris. But I met her at a cake shop when I was filling in for Iris's husband a few months ago," I say, taking them back to the starting line. "And we had a fun conversation then. Maybe a month or two later, I was on my way to the arbitration hearing, and I hopped onto the sidewalk to avoid a truck."

Axel shakes his head, huffing. "Cyclists on the sidewalk are the bane of my existence."

Drew grins wickedly at his cousin. "I thought bad grammar was? You were bitching about the misuse of lay and lie the other week."

"You lay an egg. You lie down in bed. It's not hard, people," Axel snarls like the malcontent he is.

"But what about laid? That's what I like to do in bed." Bryan smirks, stretching his big arms behind his head and parking them there.

"Yes, I believe we all like to do that in bed," Axel drawls.

Drew cups his mouth. "Earth to dickwads. I'm actually interested in Milo's tale of woe."

"Thank you, Drew," I say, then tell them about Stud-Muffin lunging for my bike, Veronica inadvertently flashing me her panties, us both spraying glitter on my beard, then me finding the lost earrings. "And after I returned them, we started texting, and now she's my employee."

Axel whistles, long and appreciatively. "That sounds like one hell of a meet-cute."

Bryan squeezes my shoulder protectively. "But Milo has a list a mile long of why he doesn't want to get . . ."

The sentence dies, and I follow my brother's gaze to Drew, who holds his beer, hand frozen midair.

"Are you okay?" I ask, a little concerned.

The football player blinks, then stares at me with new eyes. "I know who you are," he whispers. "You're Mister Sexy Pants."

14

YES, I AM

Milo

Drew points at me like I'm suddenly a celebrity. "You're a character in a dating column," he explains, grabbing his phone as I try to make sense of his gibberish. He taps repeatedly on the screen while talking a mile a minute. "The writer is anonymous, but she calls herself *Your Friendly Neighborhood Virgin*, and there's a guy she has a crush on who appears in her stories. His name is Mister Sexy Pants."

The hair on my arms stands on end. Is he pulling my leg? I mean, that's the kind of shit friends do to each other.

I want this to be real so badly. It's too good. Too thrilling. Too wickedly sexy. But he's got to be full of it.

"You read a column on dating and virginity?" I ask.

Drew stares at me, dead-eyed. "Try to read what

women say, and maybe you'd learn a thing or two about the fairer sex."

"Hey, now! I'm on a dating intel blackout. But that's not the point. Who is this Mister Sexy Pants?"

"*You are,*" Drew declares, plunking his phone in front of me and pointing to it.

I read the headline: **Things We Assume About Virgins**. Then the date. The piece ran the day after I crashed into her. With my breath held, I devour every delicious word. When I reach the middle, my breath hitches.

Do you remember Mister Sexy Pants? I mentioned him a few columns ago when he introduced me to the pleasures of ogling men in tight pants.

Today, I met him for real. And even though my valiant dog tried to defend me against a potential attack from his bike, and even though I accidentally flashed him my panties, he was still a perfect gentleman.

Holy shit.

That is us, all right, which makes me—I steal a glance at my tight-fitting burgundy pants—Mister Sexy Pants.

As I read on, my temperature climbs. She describes a fantasy about this gallant guy coming home from work, fucking her on the balcony, and making her a panini.

All the clues add up. She acted jumpy when I mentioned National Sandwich Day, like she'd been caught. Then, when Zara commented on my style, Veronica said pants were the worst.

Lies.

All sweet, lovely little lies to cover up her secret identity.

She's a sexy superheroine. Veronica Valentine by day, and *The Virgin Club* writer by night.

My employee has a wicked, crazy, dirty, filthy, beautiful crush on me, and she wants me to bang her on her balcony.

I figured out her secret, and it's incredible.

This is the best worst discovery of my life.

15

A GOOD BOSS

Milo

I'm still reeling in the morning. And, *reading*.

Then re-reading.

By the time I finish my morning coffee, I've damn near memorized her columns. Each one is a shot of adrenaline mixed with lust, chased by dirty dreams, then jet-fueled by my nitro horniness.

Great. Fucking great.

After I lock up and leave, I carry my bike down the steps in my building, Trudy trotting by my side. As I go, I ask myself—again—how the hell I'm going to make it through the rest of the summer, let alone today.

Outside my building, I glance at the next one over. It's a miracle I survived last night. That I didn't bust out of my home to howl under her balcony.

With the July sun beating down on my shoulders, I

stare at Veronica's deck, hoping for a glimpse of her, but she's not outside this morning.

All those evenings I walked past her, she must have been dictating her column. Like the night I swore she said *tell me what you want.*

The same words appeared in her top-five fantasies column. *A guy can say to me . . . tell me what you want. And I'll tell him. Because I've got a list, starting with my top-five fantasies.*

A rumble works its way up my chest. Possibly a growl.

"Maybe I need a muzzle," I mutter as I secure Trudy in her bike seat. Because all I want to do when I see Veronica is ask, *Can I take you home tonight and work through your list?*

But a good boss wouldn't say that.

And I am a good boss.

Swinging my leg over the bar, I settle onto my bike. Just as I set my phone in its holder, it pings with a text from Iris. **Can't wait to see you tonight, Funcle!**

I laugh at the nickname, then write back. **Give that little chunk a kiss. See you tonight, friend.**

I set an alarm to remind me to go. Iris had her baby a week ago, and I'm trekking to Brooklyn after work to see the crew. Maybe if I think about babies all day, I won't replay Veronica's columns in my head.

And maybe my bike will grow wings and fly.

With my head down, I put my focus solely on the road, then hop onto the street and navigate the perils of the New York streetscape. My thoughts clear as I battle traffic. Maybe I'll ride all day and all night for the rest of the summer. Sounds like a great coping mechanism.

I slow as I reach the Bikes and Blooms block, then jump up onto the sidewalk and off the bike so I can walk it the rest of the way. "You're going to meet little Danny tonight," I tell Trudy. "Does that make you an aunt? A dog aunt? A dog godmother?"

She wags her tongue as we roll up to the store.

"My bad. You're a dog mother," I say, but wait. That sounds ridiculous.

"I prefer dog-gess."

Veronica's pretty voice comes from behind me, knocking me right back into the danger zone. I turn around to see her walking toward the store, wearing a pink dress that swings seductively around her knees, drawing my eyes to her legs then up her frame.

Tiny blue tulips cover the fabric.

Hmm. What covers her butt?

"Like goddess," she adds, as if I'm a dumbass.

Because I am. I've been staring at her lasciviously. "Right. Yes. Dog-gess," I repeat, proving that I cannot function as a human being when I am suffering from an overload of lust.

Veronica strides up to the bike and stops in front of Trudy. "Want me to unbuckle her?"

"Sure." I'm super swift with one-syllable words today.

As she unsnaps my girl, I try to act normal. "So, you're here early." But not by much. Maybe like five minutes.

She gives me a friendly smile. "I dropped Stud-

Muffin at a new doggy daycare near here. Fingers crossed he does well."

"Or paws crossed," I say.

There. I said almost a full sentence that wasn't *I want to strip you naked.*

I'm giving myself an award.

Veronica scoops Trudy out of the seat, sets her down, then heads to the green door. Trudy follows, tongue lolling, tail wagging.

"Yeah, Trudy, that's how I feel too," I say under my breath.

* * *

I survive the first few hours of the day, but barely. I'm frayed thin, my resistance worn down to a thread. In between customers and phone calls and orders, I steal glances at Veronica in her pink dress.

She's busy all morning too, tending to a steady stream of foot traffic on National No Worries Day. *Don't worry today. Stop and smell the lilacs instead.*

As Veronica chats with a curly-haired woman who leans in close to whisper a question, I'm dying to know if the friendly neighborhood virgin is making another sex toy recommendation.

Bet she is, and I have to know if vibrators are the *gifties* mentioned in the review the other week.

Would a good boss ask that, though? Probably not.

But I can't stop this train of thought. She's a virgin with a filthy mind, and I am obsessed.

When lunchtime rolls around, I jump on the chance

to get some space. I ask Zara and Ian if they want a sandwich from the new shop down the block. After they give me their orders, I amble over to Veronica. "Want anything for lunch? There's Thai, quinoa bowls, and a new sandwich shop nearby?"

The angel on my shoulder says I'm just being a good boss, trying to feed my employees.

The devil says *no, you're trying to entrap her.*

Fucking devil knows me too well.

"Tempting. I would love some . . ." Veronica bites the corner of her lips.

Just say it. Say you like sandwiches and sex, and you want both with me. ASAP.

But then she smiles. "Spring rolls. With peanut sauce. Please."

Curses. "Coming right up," I say, then I take off.

What was I trying to do? Set a clever sandwich trap? Shout *aha, I knew it was you?*

I head down the block, pop into a couple of shops, and snag lunches. When I return to Bikes and Blooms, I hand out lunches then go straight to my office with Trudy and shut the door. I crunch into my chicken and sun-dried tomato sandwich in silence.

I'm going to need to regroup. *Immediately.*

* * *

By three, I'm no closer to a survival strategy. When the clock ticks five, Ian skedaddles, and Zara asks to leave thirty minutes early to see a friend.

"Of course," I say.

"Thanks. You're a good boss on No Worries Day," Zara says on her way out.

Her words echo.

Veronica's been jumpy at times. A little evasive. She's been hiding her identity, and that's understandable. But what if she's legit afraid I'd be pissed she writes about me? That has to be why she's danced around the sandwich topic, why she claims she doesn't have the writing gene, why she told me she was dictating a to-do list that night.

More like how to do her, and I fucking want to.

But she's probably freaked out that I'd let her go.

I need to tell her I'm not bothered by her objectification of *moi*.

Not. One. Bit.

When the last customer leaves, and I lock the door, I head over to her counter, determined to just say it. *I know I'm Mister Sexy Pants and I'm so good with it, and can we start working through your list as soon as humanly possible? Starting now. Right now.*

"Hey," I say with a smile. "Can I help you straighten up? Since I know you need to get your dog soon."

Her eyes flash with gratitude. "Thank you. I would never turn down an extra pair of hands."

Because you like a man who's good with his hands. You wrote that the day I crashed into you. You said, and I quote, "This is my fantasy, so he owns a combination bookstore and calorie-free cake shop. He's good with his hands too."

But that's not a good entry into the no-need-to-worry topic, so I click on the card reader to sort receipts. A minute later, my office phone rings, and I've been waiting for a call.

"That might be an apparel guy I need to talk to. I'll be right back," I say, then I dart into my office and answer.

It's Chet at Fletcher Parts, one of my regular suppliers. As Trudy wanders into my office, squeaking her gator, we discuss the delay on an upcoming order. I'm eager to end the call, but he's not so quick to hang up. "Hey, tomorrow we have a Bike to Work event in Central Park. We'll be passing out info on bike routes and sharing a checklist on safety procedures. You're still coming, right?"

That's tomorrow?

I glance at the calendar on my computer. Yup. There it is. Snuck up on me. But that's an important event. "Absolutely. I'll be there," I say, and when I finally escape from Chet the Chatterbox, I'm ready to fly to the Bloom side of the store. But Veronica's at my office door, hip jutting out, purse on her shoulder.

"Hey, do you mind if I take off now?" she asks, hooking her thumb toward the street.

Fuck. My heart clangs to the floor, right next to Trudy and the decimated reptile. "Of course," I say, since that's what a good guy would do.

Except, nope.

I'm wrong. Dead wrong.

It's No Worries Day.

"Veronica," I call out.

The charming, lively brunette turns around, tilting her head. "Yes, Milo?"

Ah, hell. The way my name rolls off her tongue is too much.

I'm not a good boss. I'm not at all gentlemanly when I close the distance between us and say, "I don't own a combination bookstore and calorie-free cake shop, but I'm very good with my hands."

She gasps. Her eyes widen, but the nerves I've seen before are all gone. The only thing I see now is desire.

"You are," she says, soft and sultry.

I reach for her shoulders, cupping them. Her skin is so soft, and so inviting. "I want to tell you something," I whisper, my voice a rough scrape.

"Tell me," she says, sounding as desperate as I feel.

Then, I follow the roadmap she gave me in number five in her top-five fantasies. "I thought about you all day."

She drops her purse to the floor, a few feet from my chomping dog. Then, she grabs my face and angles her head like she's about to kiss me.

Bring it on.

16

THE MILO BUFFET

Veronica

If I were making a list of my top-five risky ideas this summer, launching myself at the man who pays my bills would be one through five.

But lust is stronger than logic.

I clasp Milo's handsome face, look into his blue eyes, and I . . . pause.

Let myself experience the anticipation, no matter how foolish this choice is.

He curls his fingers more tightly over my shoulders, tension lining his body. But he waits too, patiently.

I've imagined kissing this man so many times. There are easily five hundred eighty seven dirty deeds and counting that I want to try with him. I have no clue how he connected the dots, and I don't care. My mind whirs into sensory overload. I crave his lips, hard and rough against mine, then tender and gentle, then swoony and so terribly soft I go weak in the knees. I'll take one of everything please.

But as I look into his clever blue eyes, a delicious new knowledge moves through me. I don't want Mister Sexy Pants anymore.

I want Milo Dawson—my boss, my new friend, this real man. And just like that, I restart, my overactive brain quieting at last. I run my thumb over his sandpaper scruff then bring his face closer to mine. I say hello to his mouth with mine.

His lips are pillowy soft, and he tastes fresh, borderline minty. Like he brushed his teeth after lunch. That alone is a turn-on, but so is the sound he makes as I kiss him. A low hum of vibration.

The noise flutters through me, making my skin buzz.

We bump noses, then angle our faces, finding a better position. A shift here, a move there as we discover how to kiss each other.

As I kiss Milo, I eagerly take mental notes, learning what he likes right as he learns more about what I crave. We read the books of each other's wishes. With each passing second, our kisses get better, hotter, headier.

I kiss the corner of his lips, then slide my mouth over his. He takes my bet and raises it, nipping me, then sucking gently on my lower lip.

That's so good, my whole body trembles. He curls his fingers more tightly around my shoulders, like if he travels one more inch on my body, he'll slam me against the wall and kiss me ruthlessly.

I *need* that. But first, I want *this* moment where I can

set the pace. He gives it to me, as if he's holding open the door to this kiss and letting me walk through in my own time. Slowly, taking my time, I cross the threshold, indulging in another sweep of my lips against his.

Then, once I'm inside, he kicks the door closed. As he takes over the kiss, his checked restraint unspools. He slides his hands down my arms, exploring me, and around my waist. Those strong hands curl around my hips, then dig in. His thumb presses hard into the bone, firm and insistent. I like that—the possessiveness in his touch. I break the kiss long enough to whisper a desperate command: "Kiss me more."

He groans, his blue eyes dark and fiery. His voice is a heady growl as he says, "You taste like cinnamon and dirty dreams."

I smile, feeling like the naughty girl I am.

Sliding his tongue over mine, he explores my mouth at a greedy, hungry pace. My body crackles with electricity from head to toe. I have to get closer to him, so I press flush against his toned frame. That makes me dizzy. I rub my thigh against his hard-on, like a little thief, stealing a preview of his firm length against me.

Milo laughs softly. "I know what you just did."

I laugh too. "Aren't you astute?"

"You tried to cop a feel," he says, his voice still raspy.

"Tried? I think I *did* cop a feel."

He reaches for my hand, threads his fingers through mine. Dear goddess. That feels so good, him holding my hand while he grinds his erection against my leg. He's sending me a message, too, as he goes stroking my palm, sliding his thumb between my fingers.

I swear he's saying *you can cop a feel with your hands now.*

I shudder out a breath, then let go of his hand to squeeze his hard-on.

"Fuck yes," he grunts, and that powers me on. I stroke and rub, savoring the hard ridge of his cock against my palm.

He pumps his hips once, twice. Then another time, like he's lost to the sensation.

Then, I squeeze him again. His restraint snaps, right with mine. Milo grabs my face, then backs me up against the wall right by his office. I lose hold of his dick when he pushes me against the doorjamb so it wedges into my back.

Angling his face against my neck, he drags his nose along the column of my throat, inhaling my scent.

"Ahhh," I mutter, a cross between a purr and a groan. Milo's sniffing my skin, and it's so fucking erotic.

His mouth travels to my ear where he whispers, all gravelly and a little frustrated, "Your orange blossom drives me insane."

But it's a good frustration. He's all tense and coiled. Like he might pounce on me. I hope he does. Really soon.

"I had a feeling," I say, all fizzy.

"Yeah. What was the giveaway?"

"You seem to like to smell me at work," I whisper.

He levels me with a gaze that's dark and hungry. "I want to smell you, and taste you, and kiss you all over," he says, as he stares at my mouth. "Shit. That's too much. I should stop."

He steps back, but I won't allow that—his worry. I reach out, grab the neckline of his shirt as I jerk him against me. "I like it," I say. "All of it. Everything."

"Good. That's so damn good. There's so much I want to say to you, Veronica," he tells me, his voice raw.

But he speaks with his hands instead, dragging one over the fabric of my dress, then gripping my thigh. I shiver, and I ache terribly for him too. My pulse beats savagely between my legs. I don't bother checking the time. I don't even care. I grab that wandering hand of his. "So, you're good with your hands, you say?"

His grin is wicked. "I can show you."

I clasp his hand tighter, slide it up, up, and under my skirt, then against my skin. "You better."

With a rough groan, he grazes his hand up my thigh, travels along my flesh.

I wobble.

Then, his fingers play with the waistband of my white panties. Can this moment please last all night?

The sweet, agonizing ache is incredible. I want to stretch this bliss for as long as I possibly can, and I want him to satisfy my need right now.

I just . . . *want.*

"Let me tell you, sunshine," he whispers, using the nickname that I imagined Mister Sexy Pants gave me in one of my columns. "*This* is heaven." He cups his palm between my thighs. "Right here," he rasps out, so I can't miss what heaven is to him—*me.*

He glides his fingers across the cotton panel of my damp panties. "So fucking wet," he says, with dirty approval.

"You ruined them," I whisper.

"And I have no regrets."

Funny, I don't have any regrets either, as I push his hand inside my undies. He slides his fingers where I'm desperate for him, stroking my slickness.

I shudder everywhere. Then, I clutch at his hair, kiss his jaw, and hold on tight as I ride his hand. He strokes me intently as I chase my release.

I know how to do this. I know what I want. I know just how hard and fast I need it.

And Milo reads my lust perfectly. "You want to fuck my hand, sunshine?"

I love that he asks. That he wants me to use my words.

"I do," I pant out, rocking my hips, thrusting wildly as I seek just the right angle, just the right speed.

I use his hand like it's my new favorite toy. When I hit maximum friction, I'm shaking all over, and this close to the edge. Delicious agony rushes through my cells. I grind against his hand until colors burst behind my eyes. I moan ceaselessly as he coaxes me through the finish with words like *yes, so hot, love this.*

And I love it too. This taste of reality.

But the blissfully real moment ends with the bleating of his phone. His alarm is a sheep letting out a long, unmistakable *baa* from his office.

Not to be outdone, my phone speaks up from the depths of my purse. A robotic, English voice asks, "What is eighteen percent of fifty?"

Milo blinks. "What the hell is that?"

I drop to my knees, grab my purse, and do math. It's

wretched. "So I don't ever miss a dog appointment. It's my evil alarm."

"I'll say."

"You have five seconds, or we will escalate," the British voice chirps.

"Escalate to what?" Milo asks, horrified. "Square roots?"

I wince as I fish out the obnoxious phone. "Exactly," I say, then tap in a nine, silencing the question.

Milo stares at me, bug-eyed. "You set an alarm that makes you do percentages? That's so cool."

"Percentages are the most useful adult math," I say with a shrug. "And I can't be late. The daycare closes in fifteen minutes."

A sheep baas from his office. Louder this time. "Shit," he mutters, then ducks into his office, and turns off his alarm too. When he returns to me, he says, "I need to see Iris's baby. But give me one minute, okay? I'll be right back."

He pops into the restroom. While he's gone, I adjust my dress, then tug at my panties.

But they're useless, and this is going to be the real walk of shame. I have to pick up my pooch in wet panties, then walk home. Ugh. Stilettos and little black dresses at dawn have nothing on soaked undies after a work diddle.

Note to self: Pack for work like you'd pack for a trip. As if you'll change skivvies twelve times a day.

But, as I sling my purse on my shoulder, I freeze. A wave of nerves crashes into me. Will I actually need to pack like this for work? Was this a one-time thing? What the hell happens tomorrow?

I glance around like I'll find a sign pointing out where we go next, but all I see is a wandering dog. Oh, shoot. Trudy paces by the front door, her eyes wide, saying *help me*.

I spin around, finding her leash on Milo's desk. I grab it, sprint to the cutie, and hook her up. We fly out the door. A few seconds later, she's squatting by a hydrant. True relief.

When she's done, Milo opens the door, his gaze a little awestruck. "You're definitely the dog-gess," he says, grateful.

I just smile. I don't know what to say. I usually do, but I've got nothing now, since I never imagined the reality after the fantasy—what happens after your boss fingerbangs you.

"I don't want to make you late. You need to get your dog," he says, apologetic, but what does his sorry mean?

I hand him Trudy's leash. His fingers graze mine while his eyes search my face. "I'll text you later, Veronica," he says, gently, but I don't want to read into his tone. He gestures to the store. "I should get my bike and go too."

His voice is strained. He must feel as awkward as I do. Great. Just great. Tomorrow is going to be so weird.

"Yeah, definitely," I say with extra pep I don't feel. I turn around, walking away, utterly bewildered.

Is this how hookups with off-limits guys go? Maybe this is why I've been picky. Maybe this is why I've avoided over-and-outs.

I head away from the store, unsettled.

Thirty seconds later, feet pound behind me, coupled with paws. Man and dog. Milo catches up to me. "I mean it," he says, insistent, and when he presses a kiss to my cheek, I believe him.

But as I walk away, I'm not worried about whether he'll text or not. I'm worried about what he might have to say.

17

THROW ME A BONE

Veronica

As I fly to Throw Me A Bone, the doggie daycare, I tap out a mayday to Ellie. This situation calls for backup.

Veronica: Oh, hi. How was your day? Mine was good. I sold some flowers, helped some customers, and JUST RODE MY BOSS'S HAND LIKE IT WAS A TEN-SPEED RABBIT!!!!

Ellie: Took you long enough.

Veronica: Not helpful! I work for him. Oh my god, what have I done?

Ellie: Well, I hope you *did* his fingers. But ideally, *after* you rang up the orders. Good customer service is so important these days.

Veronica: I give excellent customer service! But Ellie!!!! My boss has seen my O face. Clear your schedule tonight!

Ellie: Sounds like he's done a little more than *seen*. And obviously, I cleared my schedule the second I read the words boss and rabbit in the preview pane. This is going to be better entertainment than the next episode of *A Gentleman's Deal*.

I start to type ***I don't want to be entertaining. I want to be . . .***

But I stop writing as I race walk to Throw Me a Bone. I don't know how to finish that thought. Who do I want to be? A model employee? A responsible human being? A good girl who follows the rules?

I'm too frazzled to know.

As the sign for the doggy daycare comes into view, I erase those last words and start over.

Veronica: Thanks, Ellie. I need a friend tonight.

She sends me back an ***always*** and a smiley face.

I know this much. With Ellie, I can always be my ridiculous, messy, chaotic self, and she'll have my back.

18

A SEX ALGORITHM

Veronica

Since I don't want to be tempted to check my phone every five minutes for a text from Milo, I jam it to the bottom of my purse as I walk home with StudMuffin. When I reach my apartment, I set the device face down on the kitchen counter, then feed the little guy dinner.

Like a cool, calm gal, I ignore all screens as I change into pajama pants and yank my hair into a messy bun.

Text? What text? I'm not waiting for a stinking text. *Pfft.*

Approximately an hour and twenty-six minutes post-orgasm, I head across the hall for some girl time. I've got a bottle of wine, some fresh kale from the balcony, and my pup.

And check out my restraint—I've only peeked at my texts nine times since I left Throw Me a Bone.

Fine, nineteen.

Okay, ninety-nine times.

But I'm done checking for the night, I swear. I refuse to be Miss Obsessed With a Man. I'm twenty-six and since I haven't been caught up in a dude's orbit yet, I'm not going to let dick gravity pull me in tonight.

I set the phone to do-not-disturb mode, then knock on Ellie's door.

My friend swings open the door and sweeps out an arm, inviting me in. "Let the entertainment begin."

"I deserve that," I say as StudMuffin trots over to say hello to Gigi, Ellie's Chihuahua mix. Gigi snags a stuffed monkey from her toy bucket and noses it his way. As the two get to work shredding the primate in the living room, I join Ellie in her galley kitchen.

"I've got olives, three-seed crackers, and an arugula salad. You've got the truth serum," Ellie says, pointing at the wine as she thrusts the bottle opener my way. "Tell me everything that happened on the job today."

My jitters hit me again in full force. "I was supposed to get a job. I wasn't supposed to get a *lady job*," I say, then stab the opener into the cork with a huff.

"Oh, honey," Ellie chides, gently grabbing my wrist. "Never take anything out on the wine. Wine is always our friend."

"And I'm my own worst enemy." I meet her warm brown eyes and blurt out, "I'm a magnet, and I'm attracted to trouble."

With a sympathetic smile, she opens the wine, then pours two glasses. She slides one to me, then takes a drink of hers. "Trouble can be sexy. A lot of us are attracted to it. It's why bad boys and forbidden romances will always be popular. Not to mention secret office trysts," she says, then sets down her glass to add the kale to the salad. "Now, give me the goods. Was his hand as good as a toy?"

A shiver rushes down my spine. I dismiss my hot-mess worries for a beat because I'm dying to relive that moment. "It was like . . . he listened to my body," I whisper, as if speaking the words at full volume will endanger the memory. I'm still amazed at how Milo read the road map of me so easily. "He wasn't one of those *let me show you my best moves* kind of guys. It was like he wanted to give me exactly what *I* wanted."

Ellie sighs happily. "So he's like an algorithm who learns your sex preferences."

I laugh drily. "Yes, Ellie. He finger-fucked me like an AI web browser," I say, but then my laughter ends. Tension spreads over my shoulders. "But this is bad, isn't it? I'm practically banging my boss."

"Practically? Sounds like it was *actually*," she corrects as she grabs forks from the utensil drawer, then hands me one.

"We didn't have sex," I insist.

"Whatever helps you sleep at night." Ellie winks, then snags napkins from the cupboard and lifts her fork like she's toasting with the utensil. "Bon appétit. Now, take me back to the beginning."

Because we're classy, we stand at the counter and eat, forks diving into the same bowl as I tell her the rest of the story.

". . . And when he made the comment about running a cake shop, it was game on," I add, then take a drink of the wine. "Chardonnay. The drink of the boss-bangers."

Ellie's eyes glimmer. "Ooh, that makes me want to write a TV show called Boss-bangers. I'll star in it too."

"I'll be your story consultant, naturally."

"Of course you will," she says. Then her gaze turns thoughtful and a little faraway. Is she unhappy as an actress? Eager for something more? I stop thinking about my complicated situation and zoom in on her.

"Do you want to write as well as act?" I've always thought Ellie had many talents. "The stories you tell from the set of *Unfinished Business* are hilarious. I could see you writing a show about being on a show."

That reconnects her with the moment. "Maybe I do want to write too. I'm not foolish enough to think I can act forever. It's hard for women." Then, her smile grows. "Can we write a TV show about a female dating-colum-nist superhero? It'll be called *Adventures of a Sexpert*. Instead of a sixth sense for a crime about to happen, she'll get this tingly sensation down her spine when a woman desperately needs a sex toy to come. She'll have a tool belt full of different dildos, and she'll literally have to respond right then and there to deliver the right vibe to the woman," Ellie says.

I set a hand on my heart. "It's so true—not all hero-ines wear capes." We both crack up, and when I stop laughing, I let go of some of the who-am-I-and-what-happens-next nerves. Spending time with Ellie always centers me and reminds me what's important. Like friendship and career.

Which raises a new question. "Did I mess up *again*,

Ellie? I do work for the guy, and I want to learn from my past career mistakes. Obviously, I screwed up when I sent my column to Agnes and all of McGee Whitney Books. But was it wrong of me to write about Mister Sexy Pants once I started working for him? Does that make me a creeper or something?"

Ellie scoffs. "No! You haven't mentioned him *that* much since you started at the flower shop. You mostly wrote about him beforehand. And you two were even sexting before your job interview, so you knew from your convos that he was into you."

"And Milo's sex positive," I add, thinking about our text messages. "He's not an Agnes Millicent, wigging out over the mere mention of sex and sandwiches. That's a stroke of good luck."

Shaking her head, Ellie levels an intense stare my way. "It's not luck, Veronica. There's nothing wrong with your column. It's a part of you, and you don't have to justify it to anyone. You're allowed to have a life outside of work. And you never named him. He was an *idea* in your columns. He wasn't a traceable man."

I could kiss her for pointing that out. But it also reminds me that I don't know how Milo put two and two together.

Except, for the simplest of ways—he clearly read *The Virgin Club* and figured it out. But he'd be the only one who *could* connect the dots. He was the only person privy to the other side of the stories—the cake, and the dog lunging at the bike bit, and the flashing of my panties. The details were Easter eggs for him.

Which means I am officially not a creeper.

My defense rests.

But I still want to know everything. When did he discover the posts? What does he think of all the things I've shared? Though, I think I know, given the dark and dirty look in his eyes when he admitted he was good with his hands.

"Thanks for listening, Ellie," I say to my friend. "I definitely needed to talk through all this after the orgasm haze cleared."

"And I needed to hear the details. Now, tell me. What's next with Mister Sexy Fingers?"

My stomach flips nervously. "I don't know," I say, then return to the food. As we finish the salad, we're quiet for a few seconds, and in the silence, I can hear my answer. I take a deep breath, then say it out loud. "I like him. I want to see him again. But it's complicated." I shrug helplessly as I confess this new feeling, one that's deeper than sex and stronger than desire. "I don't want to ruin the dynamics at the store. And let's say we do it again—do we just go back to being employee and boss?"

Ellie smiles sympathetically. "This job is only temporary though. You're returning to publishing soon. So if you want more with him, are you truly risking so much?"

We only enjoyed an interlude. Maybe a night together is a reasonable risk after all.

"I do want *something*," I say, shoulders square, chin up. Already I feel lighter. It's freeing to admit what I want. These last few weeks, I've been stressed about the new job, the old job, the future job, the side job.

But I've also been wound up about defining what I want after dark.

Now I know precisely what I want.

Milo.

I haven't slept with anyone yet because I haven't met someone who excites me this much. The zing I feel with Milo is real. It's real in bed and out of bed. "But I have no idea if he wants more than one time," I say.

Ellie squeezes my thigh. "And you won't know till you tell him you do."

I shudder. "Now, that's scarier than admitting I'm the friendly neighborhood virgin."

* * *

Back home, after we've finished the wine and done the dishes, I focus on other horrifying things, like my future as an editor. Settling into my spot at the kitchen table, I check job listings in the book business. I'm into my sixth week of exile and, aside from Milo, no one has discovered my secret identity, so I decide to put out the feelers a little sooner than planned. I'll spit shine my cover letter and then send some emails.

With that decided, I pop onto my balcony, soaking in the warm July air, staring at the few stars I can make out in the city sky. But stargazing is just an excuse. Soon, I check the sidewalk, hoping that Milo might walk by.

I stay like that for several minutes, elbows resting on the railing, watching my mostly quiet block at ten-thirty at night. My phone's back on, but it remains silent in my pocket. Only a few hours have passed since I saw him. There's no real rush to hear from him.

Yet my entire column is about taking charge of desires.

And I have things to say to the man.

I take out my phone and start writing things like . . . *that was amazing, and I want to see you again, and what you did to me was better than my imagination, and are you free tomorrow night?*

I'm typing as the device buzzes. When I see his name pop into my texts, *I'm* the one buzzing.

Milo: First, is it weird that I think Iris's baby looks like an old man? Second, how did StudMuffin like his new daycare? Third, the whole time I was visiting the baby, it's possible my mind was entirely elsewhere.

I'm a little giddy. Okay, a lot giddy. I head inside and snap a shot of my dog sleeping with his tongue sticking out, then attach the pic.

Veronica: First, babies are weird. Second, see attached. Third, where was your mind?

Milo: Top of my list of questions I'd ask a dog if they could talk—*Why do you sleep with your tongue out?*

Veronica: What else is on that list?

Milo: Why did you just bark? How long did you actually think I was gone? And can you teach me how to shake like that post-shower?

Veronica: You do indeed keep lists in your head.

Milo: I told you so.

Veronica: Also, the dog water-shake is the ultimate life hack. We would never need towels.

Milo: Except to clean up the water on the floor from the water shake.

Veronica: Curses! We will never be free from the tyranny of towels.

Milo: So true. Also, your dog is cuter than a baby.

Veronica: Well, obvs. And thanks. Yours too.

Milo: And to answer your third question—where was my mind—here goes. For the entire ride to Brooklyn, then the entire time I hung out with Iris, Joel, and Danny, then the entire ride home, I replayed those fifteen minutes we spent right outside my office. Fuck, that was hot, Veronica.

My neck flushes as I replay the evening too. And since he's being open, I do the same.

Veronica: But I left you hanging. I hope you can forgive me and let me make it up to you.

With a deep breath, I read my very forward note one more time, then brace myself to take a chance. I hit send. He replies in seconds.

Milo: You can make it up to me anytime.

My smile is bigger than the sky. With my phone in hand, I dance around my apartment as I finish getting ready for bed. A few minutes later, when I slide under the sheets, I re-read his last note. It brings the tingles once again.

Except . . .

What now? Do I suggest we make plans for a second time? To "make it up to him"? Is that how flings work? Ugh. My lack of experience is catching up to me. I have no clue what to say, and I don't want to say the wrong thing. Don't want to mess up our work relationship or this new situationship. I'll have to let this simmer overnight.

Veronica: By the way, thanks for being cool about my Wonder Womaning you with my column.

Milo: I should be the one thanking you, Diana Prince. Also, Veronica? I'm about to conk out. I'll see you tomorrow, but before I crash, did you have a good night?

Oh. My. God. My chest flutters from one simple question.

Veronica: I had a great night.

Milo: Good. Me too.

I feel somewhat better, though I'm not sure I'm any closer to knowing if he's up for a hot summer fling or if tonight was one time only.

I'll find out tomorrow morning though. But at least he knows Wonder Woman's secret identity.

Like I needed any more reasons to find Milo Dawson so damn attractive.

19

PAPER AIRPLANES

Veronica

I wake early the next day to prep for the job hunt, drinking a chai at the kitchen table as I review my résumé. Then, I put the finishing touches on a killer cover letter that I'll tailor for each publishing house.

I send it to my sister, along with a note: *Can you take a look at this and let me know what to tweak?*

Her reply comes shockingly early. *Yes. Also, I'm at Big Cup, writing with TJ! Stop by on your way to work. We have news!*

That sounds promising. And a little distracting in a good way. A quick visit with my sister and her friend might take my mind off the jumping bean feeling inside me. Seeing Milo this morning will be weird, and I need an injection of normal to start the day.

After I finish getting ready for work, I cross Seventh Avenue, then pop into my sister's favorite coffee shop.

Hazel waves from a table, windmilling her arms like there's a chance I'd miss her.

I sail over and give TJ a kiss on his scratchy cheek, then hug my sister. I flop onto the extra chair, feeling warm and fuzzy to see the pair, more so than usual. "How's *Meet Cute Again* coming along?" I ask, since the two writing besties *finally* decided to co-write a book.

"Great since, shockingly, Hazel writes neurotic characters really well," TJ deadpans.

"Pot. Kettle," Hazel says to TJ.

He lifts his coffee cup in acknowledgment, takes a drink, then turns to me. "But I think it's safe to say our book is going better than the time she tried to co-write with Axel Huxley."

I snort-laugh. "Maybe because she doesn't want to bang you, TJ."

Hazel kicks me under the table. "I did not want to bang Axel," she hisses.

As he sets his cup down, TJ fake coughs, muttering under his breath, "You did."

I mime reining in a wild horse. "You wanted to ride him like a mustang, Hazel. Admit it."

TJ lifts a hand to high-five me. "With no need for a saddle."

I smack back and smack talk my sister some more. "Hazel wanted it bareback with her enemy."

She huffs, flicking her red hair off her shoulder dramatically. "And to think I invited you here to help you, Veronica. Why do I want to help you again?"

"Because you love me," I say, batting my eyelashes.

"Anyway," Hazel says, then gestures to her writing

partner, "TJ has good news and I wanted you to hear it from him."

Ooh, another injection. Shoot me up with more sunshine. "This sounds fun," I say to TJ.

"Last night, I had dinner with my editor, Amy. From Brooks & Bailey. She happened to mention they're about to post an opening later this week for a young adult editor. She's not handling the hiring, but if you want to reach out to Tiffany, you can tell her Amy Summers sent you by way of TJ Hardman," he says with a pleased smile.

Gah. I love my people. "Teen books would be so fun. You're the best," I say, bursting with excitement. "It's official."

"And you're like the little sister I never had," he says.

Hazel clears her throat. "And I'm your work wife, so wouldn't that make Veronica your sister-in-law?"

He points his thumb at Hazel. "This is why she's in charge of details in our books," he says, then he turns the conversation back around. "And one more thing. Amelia—she's a friend of my boyfriend—is a huge fan of your column and wants to get in touch with you about some kind of business opportunity. She's in a band called Ten-Speed Rabbit, so maybe that's the connection?" He shrugs.

"And what do you know? I'm a fan of ten-speed rabbits," I add boldly—no blush here.

Hazel chuckles. "Own it, girl."

"Absolutely," TJ seconds. "Anyway, I don't know what the gig is, but let me know if you want me to pass on your email to Amelia. I think her band might need help with social."

Hazel's green eyes light up as she turns to me. "I bet that's it. You're so good at interacting with column readers online, so maybe they want you to interact with fans?"

It's true I might need another side hustle. The job at Bikes and Blooms ends in a month and a half when Iris returns. If it takes me longer than that to swing a new book gig, I might need another temporary gig. Or a handful of them.

"Of course you can share my email," I say, then thank them and take off for work. In a few minutes, I'll see Milo again.

I wish I'd written a column on walking into work the morning after you walked out in soaked panties.

When I arrive at the shop, I pause and stare at the green door from the street. Here I go.

I draw a fueling breath and head inside. Milo's chatting with Zara at the bike counter, his back to the door, the dog sitting politely at his feet.

"And don't forget, we have a new shipment of bike gloves coming in today," he says. "I'm also expecting a special order of a derailleur for the new hybrid I'm building for a bike blogger. He chronicles all his bike adventures, the trips he goes on, the pictures he takes, and I want everything to be perfect for him. Can you text me when those arrive? The custom-build business is starting to take off." He sounds so hopeful. I've never heard him talk about his custom bikes like that before.

"It sure is, and I'm glad you started it last year. So I'll

tell you about your bike part if you order me lunch again," Zara says, a brilliant negotiator.

He chuckles softly. "Never stop being a comedian."

"Oh, I was serious. I'd like a roast beet with pesto. Yes, I said beet, not beef, because beef is gross," she says, then her eyes land on me. "Hey, V."

"Beets sound tasty, Zara," I say, smiling at her, but not for her.

Milo turns in slow motion, then his gaze locks with mine. His lips curve in a slight smile and a shiver whooshes down my body. I feel all loose and bendy, and I might melt right now. If he keeps looking at me like that, Zara is going to pick up on the fuck-me eyes.

I clear my throat.

"Hi . . . Milo," I say with an unnatural pause. Where's a dog water-shake when you need it? "Hey, Zara," I say, trying again to sound like I have spoken words aloud before.

"How did everything go yesterday?" she asks as she tugs a box of energy bars closer to her on the counter.

Wait. With what? With Milo slamming me against the wall? "Wh-what do you mean?" I stammer.

"With Throw Me a Bone. Did your little dude like it?" Zara asks as she grabs bars from the box to stack in a display on the counter.

"Oh, he loved it," I say, relieved. I push my purse strap up higher on my shoulder, just to keep busy.

"It wore him out," Milo adds, with another knowing smile slung my way.

Zara stops sorting, hands freezing on the bars. She arches a brow Milo's way. "How do you know?"

He clears his expression, clearly realizing his mistake. "Oh. Lucky guess," he says with a casual shrug, recovering quickly. He nods to the door. "And on that note, I'm outta here today."

Hold on. Did he just say he's taking off?

"You're . . . leaving?" I ask, like I've never heard of the concept of departures.

Trudy stares longingly up at him, and he rewards her with a pat on the head. "There's a bike-to-work event in the park. I promised Chet I'd help. So we need to go," he says, gesturing to his main squeeze.

He lifts her up, then pops her into her bike seat, and waves goodbye. In thirty seconds flat, he's wheeling her out the door.

That's it.

That's just it?

I stare stupidly at the door for a few seconds too long. I wasn't expecting a sailor's kiss, but I sure as hell didn't think he'd skedaddle like that. And I suppose what hurts too, is I thought he'd have mentioned privately to me that he had an off-site event.

But then, I don't know what to expect from a work tryst.

Or any tryst, for that matter.

I roll my shoulders, trying to let go of my expectations. Time to get to work. I head to the flower side of the store, setting down my purse in a cabinet.

"Want me to add a sandwich for you when I order?" Zara calls out. "I've pretty much got him over the barrel with bike intel. He loves those custom bikes almost as much as he loves Trudy."

There's a story there, but I don't want to pry. Except, I do want to pry. "Why's that?" I ask casually as I tie on my apron.

"He thinks it's what makes the shop stand out. He wasn't sure if he should get into them, though, since it's a lot of work and time, but I think someone gave him the kick in the pants a year ago and he's been loving it ever since. Good thing. His bikes and his dog are all he needs," she says, then dips behind the counter to hoist up another box.

Yup. His wheels and his wags.

That's crystal clear.

"Thanks for the lunch offer, Zara. But I brought a salad," I say, then I put my phone on silent.

For the next eight hours, I'll focus on the job I have. Tonight at my apartment, I'll pour all my attention into the jobs I want.

Men? Forget about them for now.

Work comes before coming.

All morning, I am lasered in on flowers and only flowers. Then, on the regal-looking blonde who strides into the shop, hair coiffed perfectly in her signature French twist.

"Blanche!" I call out, even though she's heading straight for me.

I'm surprised at how excited I am to see my former boss. But I guess if you ever have to be fired, Blanche is the one you want firing you.

"Hi, Veronica," she says warmly when she reaches the counter. One glance and I can tell there's something different about her. I'm trying to put my finger on it, but there's a looseness in her limbs, a comfort in her body.

Ohhh.

She's getting some on the reg. Good for her. I'm tempted to say *Life is better with Os, isn't it?*

Instead, I say, "So good to see you, Blanche."

I'm also chomping at the bit to ask for all the tea. Like . . . *has anyone breathed my name as the perpetrator, because I haven't caught so much as a whiff of trouble online or around my column about my other identity? And please tell me it's safe to swim in the publishing waters soon?*

But best to ease into that too.

"I'm great, and I might be in the market for flowers. Any idea where I can get some?" she asks playfully, gesturing to the cases upon cases of gorgeous blooms we have.

"Gee, I have no idea. But thanks for coming to Bikes and Blooms. What are you looking for?"

"I need about a dozen bouquets. I'm hosting a big brunch this weekend for my She Lifts group. It's for female executives in various industries who mentor other women," she says.

"Ooh, that sounds like a great group."

"It is. I'd be happy to connect you if you'd like," she says.

I blink, surprised. I thought she'd try to distance herself from me. But then, that's a matchstick reaction.

And she's never shown any indication that I'm persona non grata.

"Thanks. I'm all for networking," I say, a perfect lead-in to asking for details. But I also want to do my actual job. "Let me help you with the flowers first. What would you like? Or can I recommend some?"

She shoots me a *we've-got-a-secret* smile. "I do love your recommendations. As for flowers, what about snapdragons? They're so pretty."

"I love snapdragons, but they aren't a great summer flower. Maybe we could do some arrangements of dahlias and hydrangeas? They love the heat."

"Mmm. I do too," she says, purring. My, my, Blanche is like a whole new woman. Her skin is glowing too. I should market sex toys with its own day. Like Every Day. National Make Your Skin Glow Every Damn Day.

After I enter the details about the flowers and the delivery into the computer, I segue back to publishing. "So, did Darius get the promotion? He was a decent editor," I say, though the cloying way he spoke to me the day I was fired rankles me still.

Blanche scoffs. "Oh no, honey. He wasn't right for that job."

My lips twitch but I rein in a grin. "Really?"

"Truly," she confirms. "You were the best editor I've ever worked with. We haven't filled the position yet since Darius left."

My ears prick. "Where did he go?"

She waves a hand airily. "He went to Dunbar Loraine and took a job there working in non-fiction."

I shudder. "I love all books, but I'm a fiction gal."

"Same here," she says conspiratorially. Then she scans the store, and with the coast evidently clear, she leans in. "And I wanted you to know, everyone seems to have moved on from the incident. No one's talking about it, or you." She taps the counter. "Knock on wood."

My shoulders relax, and I let out a long exhale. "Do you think I can get a job in publishing again?"

"I think so. I hope so. And no one seems to have figured out you write *The Virgin Club*." But Blanche clearly has. I shouldn't be surprised though. She's a woman who does her research. "Has word gotten back to you?" she asks.

I shake my head. "Not a peep."

"Good. And while I'm here, I need to get a special birthday gift for my sister." Once more, she sweeps the store for spies. "In the same vein as the *helper* you suggested for me."

I rub my palms. This is a job for a *sexpert*.

But before I can get more deets on my next superheroine assignment, the bell rings, and a new customer strolls in. "I'll email you specifics," Blanche chirps. "By the way, I tell all my girlfriends to read your column. They love it."

"I'm so grateful for that." Her visit is a shot of vitamin D on a cloudy day. "Thanks, Blanche."

She leaves, and after I help a few more customers, I grab my phone from my pocket to tell Milo about the big order. He'll be happy to hear that, and it's the right thing to do. Clearly, he loves check-ins.

But when I click on my texts, there's a message from

him waiting for me, timestamped five minutes after he left this morning. My heart skips happily. Dammit. I half wish I didn't have this reaction to him when I have no clue what he wants. I open his note and read. **Hey! I didn't want Zara to catch on. But can I call you tonight?**

Ugh. Just tell me what you *do* want, Milo. Why can't he be direct and say he's dying to see me again?

I respond with a simple **of course.**

I say nothing about the big order. Maybe I'm being petty. I don't care. I want plans. Not texts.

When I arrive home that night, there's a package from Just for Her waiting for me in the mailroom. Weird. I didn't order anything, but when I go into my apartment and rip it open—eagerly—I squeal.

We thought you might want to try our new Butterfly! Let us know what you think! Love your column!
Xoxo
Angelica, Lark, and Christine
(AKA, the gals at Just for Her)

I pump a fist, then show it off to my pets. "Look who just scored a free gift," I say.

StudMuffin spins in a circle, although that just means he needs to pee. But I know he's secretly excited for me. I take him out for a walk, and when I return, I focus on the job hunt, sending the email to Tiffany at TJ's publishing house, then firing off emails to Peterson

Books, Dunbar and Loraine, Reiss and Reardon, and my sister's contacts at Lancaster Abel. I answer Blanche's note, putting together a virtual gift basket of recommendations for her sister. Amelia hasn't reached out yet, but there's a note from Bellamy asking if I can interact with readers again, since they're *salivating for me*.

Her words.

I laugh, then respond with *happily*, and pop over to The Dating Pool to answer questions. This is another shot of delicious adrenaline. I am in my element here, talking to other women.

Then, feeling energized, I grab my phone, and head to my balcony. I'll brainstorm ideas for my next *Virgin Club* column tonight. I've gotten ahead of schedule since I wrote three columns last week, and Bellamy is stockpiling them to release each week. But thinking ahead will keep my mind exactly where it should be—on my career.

Interesting topics about dating and virginity could be . . . How to Break the News to Your Date, or Wear Whatever You Want, or Other Things You Could Be Doing Tonight.

I like the first one, and I bet Bellamy will too. As I open the email to suggest that topic, my gaze catches on a flash of white in the corner of my balcony. Is that a paper airplane?

Quickly, I bend down and grab it. It's so intricate. It's not a third-grader's flying machine at all. It's origami level, with delicately folded wings, like it was engineered to reach a certain altitude.

Maybe three stories up from the street?

My heart skitters. Hope flashes bright and hot as I turn it over. The name on the side says *Miss Cute Devil Butt.*

I gasp with excitement, then set a new speed record for unfolding. There's a note on the inside.

Hi there. What are you up to tonight? Have I told you I make excellent sandwiches? If you want one, call me.

20

THE PRICE OF ADMISSION

Veronica

Twenty minutes and a quick shower later, I'm rushing to the door to answer Milo's knock.

When I open it, he's looking like he freshened up too. The ends of his hair are wet. His dark blue eyes lock with mine. I stare at his inviting mouth for a beat, but my eyes are eager to check out all of him, so my gaze takes a stroll. He wears a trim maroon T-shirt and skinny shorts that make me want to rename him Mister Sexy Shorts too. But off with his clothes, I say! I am going to strip him naked so damn soon.

But first, someone has to say hello.

StudMuffin bounds over, all springy as he jumps up and down on his little back legs, barking happily. Milo bends down to stroke his head. "Hey cutie," he says. Satisfied, my dog trots away to his cuddle cup and curls into a tight ball.

Now it's my turn for attention. In the doorway, my visitor stares at me with obvious approval in his eyes. I'm wearing a simple yellow sundress and no bra. The hitch in his breath tells me he noticed the lack of confinement for the girls. "Nice dress," he says.

I gesture to his clothes. "Nice everything. But I have a question for you."

"Hit me up," he says.

"What would you have done if I hadn't found your paper airplane?"

He smiles wickedly. "I winged it your way twenty-eight minutes ago, so I'd have . . . wait for it . . . called you in two more minutes."

"Good answer," I say, then check out his hands. They're empty. I tilt my head to the side. "Where's the sandwich though?"

"Is that the price of admission?"

"I was promised a sandwich. I want a sandwich."

He wags a finger at me. "You dirty little liar. You pretended you didn't love sandwiches. Many times over. I offered you sandwiches; I confessed my love of sandwiches. And all along, you were loving on sandwiches too," he says, grinning like he's won a prize.

The prize of me. "A girl's gotta have some secrets," I say then I grab the neck of his shirt, tug him close, and shut him up with a kiss.

"Mmm," he murmurs.

The man shows off his multitasking skills next when he kisses me as he pushes into my apartment, then slams the door with his foot.

Oh, yes.

That is such a wind-me-up move. I break the kiss. "That's on a list somewhere," I tell him. "What you just did."

He cups my cheek possessively. "Good. I want all your lists, and I'll make you a sandwich later, I promise," he says, then sweeps a hot, demanding kiss against my lips.

My stomach flips. My knees weaken. I grab the neck of his shirt to hold on tighter.

He pushes me against the wall in my foyer, then drops his face to my neck, dragging his nose along my skin, drawing in a deep hit of me like he did yesterday. "Your scent is in my head," he says, rough and hungry. "All day long. Is it your lotion? Or shampoo? Or just you?"

"Lotion," I murmur, my hands traveling up and down his chest, exploring his pecs over the fabric of his shirt. I want him to take me against the wall. Slam my wrists over my head, yank up my skirt, tear off my panties . . .

But there's something wet on my ankles.

Familiar too.

I break the kiss, dropping my gaze. Hot Stuff is licking my ankles. Milo chuckles as the cat finishes his feast, then sashays away, tail twitching saucily as he disappears into the living room.

"He likes your lotion too," Milo says.

"He also loves my hair. He rubs against my head whenever he can."

Milo wiggles a brow, then slides up against me, rubbing his face against my hair. "Smart cat."

"You might think that's funny, but your face in my hair turns me on," I whisper.

"Everything you do gets me hard," he says.

I gasp. Heat pools between my legs from his base words.

He pulls back, looks me in the eyes. His gaze is electric but vulnerable too. "Want to know why I took off so quickly this morning at work?"

"I do."

"I didn't want to make it too obvious at work that I was dying to see you. I wasn't sure if you wanted anyone to know. And once I saw you, I had to get the hell out of there or everyone was going to be able to tell how much I want you," he says, making my silly heart dance.

"I get it," I say, playing with the hem of his shirt.

"And I didn't want to explain all that over text. I just wanted to tell you in person."

"We had a big flower order today," I say, adding a confession of my own. "I wanted to tell you over text, but I didn't know . . ."

"If I wanted to see you again?" he finishes, his tone gentle.

"Yes," I admit softly. He's easy to talk to. He's so open, so non-judgmental.

He lifts my chin. "Have I mentioned I thought about you all day?"

"Maybe," I say, fighting off a smile.

"Veronica," he begins. "I want you so much."

Those words are a blast of lust. I nibble on the

corner of my lips as desire swallows me whole. "Will you fuck me tonight?"

He growls a *yes*.

One minute later, we're on my balcony, my ass up against the brick wall, my fingers roaming over his scratchy beard. Milo cups my tits as we kiss ruthlessly, him grinding against me. It's mind-blowing, the friction. Everyone should be kissed like this. Hell, the skyscrapers are jealous. The Brooklyn Bridge is getting turned on. The stars are horny.

He squeezes my nipples, and I am liquid everywhere. My bones melt right along with my panties. I need them off, like, yesterday.

"Milo," I murmur.

Breathing heavily, he pulls back. "Yeah?"

"Go down on me," I instruct, feeling powerful as I tell him what I want, feeling grateful that he's the right man to give it to me.

His eyes pop. They twinkle with *wows*. "You're killing me, sunshine," he mutters, then sinks to his knees.

No one can see him. With the solid brick wall, I'm only visible from the waist up.

He pushes up the skirt of my dress, and drops his head back, laughing.

He hooks a finger through the waistband of the white cotton. "Skulls," he says, admiring the cartoon illustrations on the fabric. Then he whispers the word again—*skulls*—as he presses a kiss to the cotton. I moan when he pulls off my panties, tosses them behind him on the patio, and brushes the softest, most tender kiss to my center.

The sound he makes is devastating. It's better than a fantasy. It's all real, and soon he's exploring me with his lips and tongue.

I'm not sure how I'm standing. I ache tremendously between my thighs. But he soothes the ache with an eager mouth and strong fingers that dig into the flesh of my ass.

Soon, I'm louder than an ambulance siren in New York City.

"Yes, that, so good," I say, like a dirty chant as I clutch at his hair.

As he consumes me, he brushes his beard against my thighs, then sucks on my clit.

I can't take it. I can't withstand the pleasure, the decadent assault on my senses, the utter intensity of his soft, insistent mouth.

It's too much, and I'm gone, spiraling into a terrific orgasm. I whimper and moan quietly. I don't want the neighborhood to hear me come.

Just him.

Only him.

This handsome, clever, caring man kneeling before me, worshipping my body with his wicked mouth.

When I come down, I exhale several staggered breaths, then offer him a hand to pull him up. "Rolling off the tongue is so important," I whisper as he stands.

"It's a vital skill that must be practiced daily," he says with a smirk.

Daily practice with him is dangerously enticing. I

think I want that. But first, I need the rest of tonight. "Inside. Now. I want you naked."

He scoops me up, tosses me over his shoulder and carries me inside. When he drops me on my bed, he braces himself on his palms and gazes down at me. "Look, sunshine. This is going to be fucking amazing for me no matter what. So I want you to tell me exactly how you want me to fuck you. Tell me what position you want. How hard, how gentle, how dirty. I've read every single word in every single column of yours. I've loved them all. I know you've got a million fantasies in that beautiful mind of yours, and I want to give them to you," he says. "Every. Last. One."

I do have countless dirty dreams, but Milo's just given me a new one—I want a man who studies my desires and is devoted to delivering them. I loop my hands around his neck. Feeling free and fearless with him, I let him deeper into my mind. "In my head, we've fucked so many times," I say.

He grunts, low and carnal, then crushes his lips to mine. We kiss in a frenzy, making out as we tug at clothes, toss garments on the floor.

Then, he stands and he's naked in front of me. He's down to nothing, all toned and inked and steely hard.

I sit up, my breath coming fast.

This is real. This is happening. I'm about to do something I've only ever thought about. I swallow roughly, a little uncomfortably. Sex in my head has been hot and electric with perfect moves, no pain, no conse-quences.

But Milo's a real man, with a heart, and a mind. Will

I like it? Will it hurt? And will I make him lose his mind? I want him to feel incredible too. That's why my heart is beating rabbit-fast. He's so much more than a distant crush.

And I don't know what to do next.

As if he's reading my nerves, he reaches for my hand. "You okay, sunshine?"

I nod nervously, taking his offer. Our fingers thread together. "Mostly," I answer.

"Then we'll wait till you're *completely*," he says.

I can't handle all the feelings flooding me, so I zero in on the physical as I pull him down on top of me. "Kiss me nice and slow," I say, hoping a kiss erases the last remnants of my butterflies.

"Anything you want." Slowly, he rests his body on mine. He whispers gentle, tender kisses on my mouth, my neck, and in the hollow of my throat.

Then, I swear, he sees my soul when he says, "We don't have to do a thing if you don't want to." He rolls off me and runs a finger down my arm. "Want to get something to eat and watch TV instead? Or we could go for a dog walk. There's a cute café in Chelsea. Pups and Cups. We could take our dogs there and get a late-night latte."

He's so earnest, so sweet, and my heart thumps.

I had no idea I needed that invitation. That *out*. Of course, I can give it to myself. I can stop at any moment. But his willingness to spend the evening clothed or unclothed jumpstarts me again. I reach for a condom from the nightstand drawer, but he's faster to the draw.

Reaching for his shorts on the floor, then grabbing one from his wallet.

I straddle Milo. "I want to ride you. There's no *mostly* anymore."

"Good," he says with a grin, then parks his hands behind his head, his smirk crooked and sexy. "Then put that on me."

I grip his shaft, sliding my hand up and down his hot, velvet length, recording every sharp inhale of breath he takes. Then I open the condom, roll it down, and climb over him.

He grips my hips, his eyes locked with mine. Those dark blues flare with desire, but tenderness too.

I shudder everywhere, one hundred percent back in the sex zone. Here, I know what I want. His desire. His words. "Tell me what *you* want," I demand. "Say it."

He rumbles. "Get on my dick, sunshine, and take me for that ride."

My body heats like a supernova as I rub the head of his cock across my wetness. Then, I guide him into me.

"Ohhh," I whisper as I take him in an inch, maybe more.

"Yessss," he mutters, his eyes slamming shut.

That. That unfettered reaction spurs me, and I sink down, wincing as I go.

He opens his eyes. "You okay?"

"I am," I say. It's true enough. I'm full of sharp edges and rough corners as my body stretches in new ways. The fullness is strange and new, and almost too much.

Until . . . his hands slide along my stomach, and he

cups my breasts then sits up. His face is inches from mine. His eyes spark with passion and something else.

Longing, maybe? Unexpected emotion? I hope so.

I don't think this is just sex for him. I don't know what *it* is, but I'm almost sure it's more than sex for both of us.

That knowledge thrills and scares me.

But mostly, it excites me.

I lean in and kiss him. Then I start to move, and as I go, all the edges burn off. All the corners melt.

I'm warm, and everything is wonderful as I fuck Milo, and he fucks me, and we move together.

But there's one little thing that would make this moment even more wonderful.

21

AN ALLIGATOR PIT

Milo

This is the best view in the history of the world—Veronica riding my cock, her tits bouncing, her neck flushed.

I dig my fingers harder into her hips. My jaw is tight, and I fight off the onslaught of pleasure.

But it's hard, it's so damn hard when she pushes me down on the mattress, parks her hand on my chest, and says, "I want to use a toy too. Do you—"

"Do it. Fucking do it," I say before she can even finish asking *do I mind, do I care, would my fragile male ego be hurt if she wanted a little help from a friend.*

Fuck. No.

"Can I get one for you? Where are they?" I ask, so damn eager to help send her over the edge.

"Nightstand drawer," she says on a harsh pant.

I reach over, yank it open, and blink at the overflowing stash of vibes of all sizes. "It's a battery-operated bonanza," I say.

"Damn right it is." She stretches, grabbing one. A tiny black thing. With the finesse of an expert, she punches a few buttons, then slides it between her legs, and strokes her clit as she rides my dick home.

I stand corrected.

This is the best sight ever. Veronica, using my dick as a toy right along with her magic speeding bullet as she trembles all over. Her lips part, and her throaty moans light a match inside me. My vision blurs, and then I'm coming hard with her. I can barely catch my breath it's so good. She's moaning for days too, as she falls onto my chest, and we breathe out hard together, the blissful collapse after the finish line.

When I get my bearings, I thread my fingers into her hair and bring her close for a kiss.

She smiles against me, sighing blissfully.

Then, I notice a faint buzzing, and I glance down at the purple duvet. The black bullet is bouncing happily on the cover, still going, so devoted to the task.

As I watch it with a dopey, post-sex smile, the most surprising thought lands in my brain.

I want to see that image again and again, here on her bed, in her home.

But, as I wrap my arms around her, maybe that's not so surprising. Scary, but not surprising.

* * *

Sometimes, you just want to curl up on the couch after sex, skim little kisses along your lover's neck, and whisper sweet nothings.

Or cook for her, then watch a good flick.

I mean, I *think* those are all the standard post-sex activities. But I'm a dog person, and so's Veronica.

I'm in the bathroom after cleaning up when I look down to see StudMuffin staring at me ominously. Tick tock. I tug on my shirt. His big brown eyes are imploring. Oh man, I know that look. I zip up my shorts and drag a hand through my hair, calling to Veronica in the bedroom where she's getting dressed. "Sunshine, you want me to take the dog out?"

She pops her head out the door, tugging her sundress over a pair of fresh undies as she surveys the scene. "I'll go too." Then her brow knits. "What about Trudy? Want to get her?"

My heart gives a kick. "Let's walk the beasts. Meet you outside in two minutes," I say, then take off to get my girl next door.

One hundred twenty seconds later, Veronica pushes open the front door of her place and bounds down the steps with her little blond monster. After the dogs give each other a quick hello, we walk them down the block on a summer evening.

Veronica hums happily, and that's a damn good sign. I always want to make a woman happy, but it's best to ask "was it good for you" in some form or another.

"I have another question—"

We each gesture awkwardly to the other. "Go ahead," I say as the dogs stop at a tree and do their business.

"You go first." She sounds a little hesitant. Maybe she needs me to be the one to dive into a postmortem. I get that.

I inhale, but when the question forms in my head—*was that good for you*—it seems callous, something a dude might say to a hookup right before he's out the door with a dismissive *see you around*, already knowing he'll ghost her.

The thing is—I will see Veronica around. Dating might suck more than subways, but I don't want to make Veronica feel like a hookup.

Clearing my throat, I start over as we resume our pace. "So, if memory serves, we've got soap and grammar as two things we both love," I begin. "Have we found a third?"

Smirking, she steals a glance at me as we turn onto Hudson Street. "Milo, are you trying to get me to admit I, too, love sex?"

I gasp in exaggerated surprise. "Me? Never."

"Good. I didn't think that was your style, to fish for a compliment," she says.

God, she's adorable, thoroughly and completely.

But . . .

Was I fishing for a compliment? Hell, I fucking was. Screw the games. I turn to meet her gaze and cliff-dive into the dangerous waters of opening my heart. "You're incredible. Sleeping with you was amazing. I hope you liked it half as much as I did," I tell her as we slow our pace in front of a trendy bar serving designer cocktails.

With the dog leash curled tight in her hand, she leans in close, dusts a kiss along my jaw, rubbing her face against my beard. "I did love it," she says, no teasing, no sarcasm. "I want it again."

"Me too." I kiss her, then tip my forehead to the bar. "Get a drink with me. They have good tapas too."

She narrows her eyes. "Are you trying to get out of making me a sandwich?"

I drape an arm around her shoulders. "Only because I want to sit outside on a summer night with you."

I don't say *I want to have a date with you*. She's a smart woman. She can figure it out.

Ten minutes later, we're drinking mojitos and noshing on quesadillas at an outdoor table, dogs at our feet.

She holds up a pepper quesadilla. "If you think about it, this is really a tortilla sandwich."

"Does it count, then, toward the price of admission?" I ask, taking a bite of another one.

"It seems you've fulfilled your paper airplane promise," she says.

I smile, enjoying New York under a hot summer night sky with the virgin next door who's not a virgin anymore. That deepens my smile, but reminds me she'd wanted to ask me something too. "We never got back to your question earlier?"

She looks me square in the eyes. "When did you figure it out? That you're Mister Sexy Pants?"

I'm happy to share. I think she'll appreciate the story. "I told some friends about you over the weekend when we were playing Skee-Ball. One of them happens to read your column, and since I mentioned our dog-meets-bike-meets-your-devil-butt incident, he figured out I was the guy in your columns."

Her eyes flicker with wonder, perhaps. "One of your friends reads *The Virgin Club*?"

"He said it's required reading for dudes who like chicks," I say.

"That's awesome. I didn't know I had many male readers," she says. She takes a drink, her expression still one of delight. That makes me happy—that I gave her that little boost simply by letting her know she has a fan.

"And Drew made it clear he thought it was ridiculous that I didn't read it. But I went on a dating intel blackout after my ex," I say. We're going to have to talk about the ex situation at some point, and it might as well be now.

"The one who tried to steal StudMuffin's new crush?" Her eyes drift down to my brown and tan girl, lounging under the table. Veronica's little dude is making heart eyes at Trudy while pawing at her, all *look at me* style.

Such a typical man.

I tear my gaze away, returning to the unpleasant but important topic.

"Callie and I split up almost a year ago when I found out I was one of not two, not three, but four boyfriends of hers."

"Wow," Veronica says, awestruck.

I'm still a little embarrassed. Maybe I always will be. "I guess I got hoodwinked," I deadpan keeping my tone light despite that whole clusterfuck. "She scammed money out of her exes and me. Some of them assumed I was in on her lies and got revenge by leaving nasty online reviews for the shop. By the time I got out of the relationship ten or so months ago, I was surly and unhappy."

"I don't blame you. That sounds terrible," she says.

"It was not a good time in my life. On top of losing Trudy for a while," I say, shuddering. "Bryan suggested maybe I needed to take a good, long timeout from dating. Who knows how long. But I removed all apps. Everything but the store's social media. My mom said the same thing—to take some time to heal," I add.

"That's solid advice. Moms are good like that," Veronica says with a smile.

"I think so, but it also comes from her experience," I say, and wow, I did not plan to dive headfirst into the how-did-your-parents-mess-you-up convo, but here I go. "My dad cheated on her a bunch of times. She told me later that when she finally found out, she'd needed some time to *detox*. Her words."

"That makes a lot of sense," Veronica says, full of understanding. "Sometimes we need to lick our wounds."

"Yeah, it takes a while. I'm still working on it," I say. It's best to share the score, and I could go on but I've said enough. It won't do any good to add that I still don't know if I can trust my radar. I'd completely missed any signs from Callie, and look how that played out. I nearly lost my little cutie. I bend down and give Trudy a necessary pet. I missed her so much.

"Online dating is supposed to make things easier,

but it makes it harder in some ways," I say. "Since it's easier to lie."

"It's a swamp out there, isn't it?" Her gaze turns thoughtful as she stirs her drink. "Honestly, I think that's why I stayed a virgin so long."

Oh, yes. Keep talking, honey. This is so much more interesting than my year off the market. "Because dating is another word for disaster?"

She gives a humorless laugh but nods. "I was at a bar with Ellie a few months ago, watching a Comets baseball game, and some guy next to us made a comment about how he was surprised I knew sports. I asked, 'Because I'm a woman?' And then he said, 'You don't have to be a bitch.' Boom, just like that he went to the name-calling. But then he picked up some other woman afterward, someone who didn't care he'd called me a bitch, and took her home. My sister writes romance for a living, and she's always talking about characters' emotional wounds, and I'm telling you, modern dating is one giant emotional wound," she says, shaking her head like she still can't believe what a mess the world is.

"I'll drink to that," I say, knocking back some more of the cocktail. "Dating is an alligator pit. So that's why you waited?"

"Yes, but there are other reasons too." She takes a drink, giving me flirty eyes over the top of her glass. When she sets it down, she finishes with, "I'm picky."

Her words thrum through me, making the hair on my arms stand on end. "And you picked well," I say, then I dip my face to hers and brush a soft, barely-there kiss to her minty, mojito-y lips. When I pull back, I add softly, "Good thing we met in real life then, instead of online."

It's flirty but true. We click so damn well in person.

But she sits up straighter like I said the wrong thing. "Do you think I lied to you about my column?"

With a pang of sympathy, I shake my head. "Sunshine, you're not a liar. It was hot, the way you kept your secret identity on the DL."

She laughs, clearly relieved. "Just like Wonder Woman, only I was saving the world one sex column at a time."

"Seriously. You have no idea how unbelievably sexy it was to discover what was in your columns. I kind of went up in flames. I was like a GIF of a man on fire."

She lifts her glass and clinks it to mine. "It was pretty sexy writing about Mister Sexy Pants. The times I got off thinking about you . . ."

I groan. We've got to get out of here ASAP, but first things first. "I noticed you had a list of fantasies in your columns," I say, having memorized all those gorgeous lists.

She runs her finger along the rim of her glass. "I did."

A serious relationship is a no-go. But tackling a sex list of fantasies with this fantastic woman who loves all the same things I do?

"Want to work through some of them?"

Please say hell yes.

"With you?" she asks, all innocence.

I roll my eyes. "I'll spank you for that."

"That's on my list somewhere. Among other things," she says, then leans in close to whisper in my ear.

* * *

Twenty minutes later, we're back at her place. I'm on her couch, my knees spread, her face between my thighs. I spear my fingers through her messy chestnut locks.

Her lips are *Come to Bed Red*. She applied lipstick on the way home, and I'm wiping it off with my dick.

"Fuck, you look good, sunshine," I tell her, grunting as she runs her tongue along my shaft, then draws my cock back into the paradise of her mouth.

I'm this close to coming again.

Then Veronica slinks a hand between my legs, tugs on my balls and presses a finger against my ass.

Holy fuck.

It's a blizzard in my brain. I go blind with pleasure as my hips jerk up and I growl, coming down her throat.

I'm panting, buzzing, and not sure my feet will touch the ground for days.

But eventually, when I come down to earth, she's smiling at me like the devilish angel she is. "Told you I'd make it up to you," she purrs.

"You're right. You're always right," I say, then I catch a glimpse of Trudy, since the door to the bedroom's open. My girl's made herself at home on Veronica's bed, sleeping soundly on a pillow.

"I think my dog wants a sleepover," I say, hope bouncing around in my chest as I wait, like a dog, for an invitation.

I'm desperate to curl up with Veronica and feel her against me all night long. And in the morning too.

"Is she the only one?" she asks, that same hitch of hope in her tone.

I gently tug her up and onto my lap. "No. I do too because then I can wake you up with my mouth on your delicious pussy," I whisper, sweetening my invitation.

"Good thing tomorrow is National Have Peaches for Breakfast Day," she says, and I crack up.

After we brush our teeth and say goodnight to our pets, I haul her into bed.

We dim the lights, and she shifts to her side. "You've already knocked off three items from my original top five."

I count on my fingers. "I made you laugh, I made some noise, and I told you I'd thought about you all day. So we've only got two left?" I ask, offering all the prayers to the dirty gods that she's got an endless list somewhere.

"Please," she scoffs. "I made a new list."

And I've got a new temporary lover.

22

HE ROSE TO THE OCCASION

Veronica

Since Wednesday is hump day and I'm feeling a little sassy—or maybe a lot—I decide to surprise Milo. A few minutes before the shop opens, I pop outside with the chalk and make a declaration on the board.

I stand back and read my new slogan under the bright morning sun. I am seriously pleased.

Milo must catch sight of me through the window because he strides outside, question marks in his eyes. He scans the sidewalk, but no one else from the store is in earshot. "You look very cat-who-caught-the-canary-of-a-cock."

I laugh, shaking my head at his ridiculousness. "Yes, the *only* reason I could be grinning is that I like your dick."

He gives a confident shrug. "I thought so."

I step aside and sweep out my arm to show off my handiwork.

National Hump Day. You rose to the occasion, right?

Laughing, he drags a hand down his face. "A dirty mind is a terrible thing to waste, and you don't waste it," he says, admiringly.

"It's not too much, is it?"

He scoffs. "No way. Business has been up since you started your campaigns."

Business goes up today too. We sell out of roses in a few hours, so I have to change the slogan that afternoon.

Get tulips for the one you want to kiss, and yada, yada, yada.

I'm finishing up with a customer when a mom I recognize from the Little Artists class pops into the store. Ashlee's on the marketing team at The Dating Pool, and I've met her once or twice when I've been to the offices, so our worlds already collided. "I could not resist. I have to snag some tulips for my wife," she says. "Especially since the kiddos will be at your class tonight, which gives us a free hour."

Wink, wink, indeed. "And I trust you'll use it well," I say.

"We love your column but especially the reader comments. That's my favorite part—the Q and A," she adds. "We read it after the kids go to bed, of course."

"So glad to hear that," I say as I ring up some bright red buds.

"And I'm trying to decide if I want the new butterfly vibe from Just for Her," she says, and I love how bold she is, asking for sex-toy advice as she shops. "It's pricey. I can't decide if I want to spring for it."

I beckon her closer. "The company just sent me one. For free. Gah. I'm still dancing."

She gasps. "You have arrived."

I preen a little. "It might have been one of the greatest moments of my life. But I need to test it solo. Last night, I used another one."

One well-groomed eyebrow arches. "Did I just hear *last night I used another one . . . with a man?*"

Ohhh. I suppose that cat's about to come out of the bag in my column. I give a coy smile. "I sure did. Man and vibe. And it was soul-shattering."

She beams. Then she blinks. "Wait. Hold on. Does that mean . . . ?"

She sounds worried, so I toy with her for fun. "That I have to retire?" I ask with a frown.

"Well, do you? Please say no, please say no."

I smile. "My editor and I discussed *my status* when I started the column. We'd just change the name to *The Virgin Club Alumni.*"

Ashlee laughs. "Get it, girl."

She takes the tulips and goes. A few seconds later, Mister Big Ears strides over. "Should I add toys to the inventory?"

"Maybe you should," I say playfully, then furrow my brow. "Do you want me to stop talking about them when customers ask?"

"Hell no. I might even change the name to Bikes, Blooms, and Buzz." He steals a glance at the bike side of the shop. Zara and Ian are busy with customers, with

James working on a bike, so Milo lowers his voice. "When can I see you tonight? I've got my palm ready and willing to smack your gorgeous ass."

With a devious glint in his eyes, he lifts his right hand and mimes swatting, and I laugh.

"Oh, you won't be laughing later," he teases.

"Good," I say, my stomach flipping. Then I turn serious. "I have to teach my Little Artists class on Christopher Street. I should be done by seven-thirty," I say, and I'm about to suggest we meet at my place at eight-thirty or nine, but Milo says, "I'll pick you up after class if you'd like. We can get a bite to eat first."

Tingles whoosh down my chest. I wasn't expecting a date or a pickup. But I am not turning them down. "Sounds perfect."

* * *

I'm not feeling so perfect that evening when I check my email as I head to class. Walking up Seventh Avenue, I read a note from Peterson Books for Young Readers, thanking me for my résumé and saying it's on file. My shoulders sink. That's a shame, because Peterson had posted a specific job opening I was more than qualified for. It's strange that I wouldn't even get a personal reply, and my stomach twists with worry. Then it knots tighter when I read the next email. It's from Reiss and Reardon, and it's an automated message—*we have no openings at this time.*

But that's not true. Reiss had an opening as a middle grade editor, and while it was an executive editor job that I'm probably not qualified for, it was still an opening. This email feels like a lie, but it's not as if I can point fingers at this generic HR reply.

When I reach the community center, I do my best to put the nagging fears out of my mind as I go inside, head to the art room, and smile for the kids. "Who wants to create today?"

The beaming faces of the kiddos help me ignore my woes for the next hour as we work on collages, sprinkling some with glitter.

When class ends and I've cleaned up, the head of the community center walks out with me. "Looks like your new gig is going great," Jessica says with a curious glint in her dark eyes.

"It is. I'm enjoying it," I say. That's all true. It's been the temporary gig of my dreams, but the bike and flower shop is not *hashtag life goals*.

"I got a new bike there a couple weeks ago, and I saw your sign out front, then checked out each new one after that on social. So clever. Would you ever be interested in doing some social for us? For pay, of course."

Wow. I wasn't expecting that. I don't see myself as a social media strategist, but I won't turn down good side gigs. "Sure. I'm open to that," I say cheerily.

"Cool. I want to expand our marketing. I'll reach out soon."

"Great," I say, then a flash of a sexy silhouette catches my gaze. I can't help but smile when a bearded man in slim-fit shorts and a casual green polo waves from the sidewalk. I beckon him up the steps. "This is Milo. He owns Bikes and Blooms," I say, introducing them. "This is Jessica. She runs Little Artists, and she got a new bike from your shop a few weeks ago."

"Sweet," he says, shaking her hand. As they talk wheels for a minute, my mind returns to the emails. Will other publishers decline so quickly? I still haven't heard from Tiffany, TJ's contact. But maybe I will soon. I draw a deep breath, trying to ease my anxiety.

I reconnect with Milo and Jessica's conversation as they talk about an upcoming charity ride Milo plans to do. "One of my business partners asked me to join his team," he says.

I paste on a smile so they don't think I went to la-la land.

Jessica turns to me but wags a finger at Milo. "And don't you dare let her go, but I might want to steal her away every now and then to do some social media for us. National Pajama Day was my favorite."

Milo deals me a smile that feels both personal and professional. "Thanks. Veronica is a rock star," he says.

His professional praise is a welcome counterbalance to the two rejections. But I'm still not ready to think about a future in social media.

We say goodbye, then Milo and I dart a few blocks over to Charles Street.

After we grab a table at a Middle Eastern café, ordering falafels and hummus, I zoom in on him, pushing the book business as far away as I can. "What's the bike ride you're doing? And is that why you like sexy pants—because you're so used to tight bike shorts?" I ask, cradling my chin in my hand.

He glances down at his shorts. "I like clothes. I'm just

not one of those Levi jeans-and-gray-shirts guys," he says, giving a simple answer that I adore.

"Hallelujah."

"I'd say, since my clothes got you to notice me," he says, with a crooked smile. "Anyway, Chet from Fletcher Parts is doing a two-day ride this weekend. It's a charity fundraiser, and he has room on his team. So I think I'll join him, and maybe convince some of my buddies too. The cause is near and dear to my heart."

I sit up straighter, eager for details. I want to know more about the man. "Is it an animal rescue?"

"Actually, it's for a crisis hotline and online support groups for anxiety and depression. My mom works in the field, and I just think mental health doesn't get enough attention. I've always tried to help raise awareness when I can."

My heart warms, thumping harder. "That's lovely. Is that why you say it's near and dear? Because of her work?"

"Definitely. I personally haven't struggled with those issues, but she really helped my brother and me when we were growing up to see the scope of things people deal with and their different coping mechanisms. Back in high school, I helped out with some groups that tried to raise awareness for teen mental health, then in college too. So it's always something I've done," he says.

"You're an ally," I say.

"I try," he says with an easy shrug.

My heart flutters, and I dip my face.

"Why are you being all shy?" he asks.

I wave a hand, trying to dismiss my reaction. "Maybe just stop being so . . . yummy," I mutter.

With a soft laugh, he presses his forehead to mine. "Sorry, not sorry. That'd be impossible. I'm delectable and you know it."

But he's also unavailable. Last night, he said he was taking a hiatus. He didn't say his timeout had ended, but he didn't have to. The implication was there—he's still detoxing and knowing how off-limits he is hurts a bit. Though I get it. I *have* to get it. And maybe his status frees me to say the next thing. "You sure are."

Since I know we're going nowhere. Which means I better embrace every second of our to-do-list days.

When the food arrives and we tuck in, Milo gestures down the street toward Little Artists. "What Jessica suggested—is that something you want to do? Social media?"

"I don't know. I haven't thought about it before. I really want to return to publishing, but I got two rejections today," I say, as I slice a chunk of the falafel then dip it into the hummus.

He frowns. "That stinks. But there have to be more jobs out there."

"There are, but it's a small field. There aren't many publishing houses, and I'm a little worried I might never get a gig," I admit.

"Why's that?" he asks, concerned as he swipes a pita through the hummus.

I set down my fork, then rip off the Band-Aid and tell him the full story of the night of my mortification.

He looks horrified for me, muttering *whoa* after *wow* after *holy shit*. "Sunshine, your cat's a dick."

"But it's my fault. I should have been more careful."

He cups my cheek, shaking his head. "We all make mistakes. Look at Callie and me. The key is learning from them."

I believe that. I am trying to learn from my mistake. But what is the lesson? Be more careful? Trust my instincts? I'm not sure, honestly. "You're probably right," I say, half-heartedly.

"Listen, I have faith you'll get interviews soon. And I'd be happy to fill in for you if you needed to go during the workday. I can even ask Iris if I can't make it. I bet she'd come in for an hour or so."

"You'd do that?" I ask.

"Of course," he says with a crisp nod. "You'll get back into children's books. Just like I'll keep expanding in custom bikes."

"Is that your dream?"

His blue eyes twinkle as he tells me more about the custom ones he's built, his thrill in crafting them, the reception they get. He's lit up in a whole new way, and I love how he's letting me into his mind and his soul.

I love too that when the meal ends, he bends close to me to whisper, "You know what's next?"

I shiver. "I'm pretty sure I do."

23

TWO DOWN

Veronica

I'm on all fours, wearing my birthday suit and Milo's handprint on my ass. His other hand is wrapped in my hair, and he is fucking the hell out of me.

It's punishing in a dizzying way.

The pace, relentless. The smacking, loud. The hair pulling, bordering on painful. And I am lit up. Pleasure coils in my center. He drives deeper, grunting with every rough thrust. "Fuck, you feel so good," he groans.

"So do you. But I want it harder," I beg.

He growls, low and animalistic. "My cock or my hand?"

"Both," I answer, and a roar rips from him.

He snaps his hips, fucking me ruthlessly while swatting my ass. A delicious burn sears through me, a warning sign that I'm close. I slide my hand between my legs, stroke my clit with a few fast flicks of my fingers, and then pleasure bursts, diamond bright.

Everywhere.

In every single cell.

Seconds later, he shouts *coming*, then he stills and shudders.

Spent, we collapse onto the bed, panting.

Gently, he eases out and flops next to me. He's shaking his head, amused. Maybe amazed?

"What is it?" I ask, curious.

"Your sex drive is the greatest gift ever," he says, then kisses my cheek.

I just smile. "So's yours."

He drops a kiss onto my lips. I sigh, happily but wistfully. I'll miss his kisses when this ends.

I'll miss them a lot.

* * *

Later, after we take out the pets, I show Milo my favorite books that I've edited. But when I remember my promise to Ashlee, I drop the book I'm holding and turn to Milo with a wicked smile.

"What's that for?" he asks, pointing to my mouth.

I wiggle my brows. "Want to watch me . . .?"

The sound he makes sends shivers over my skin.

I grab the Butterfly, settle back on the pillows, and push off my panties. Then, I play with the toy for long and luxurious minutes until I send myself over the edge.

I've done this many times, but never for an audience. It's better with his eyes on me the whole time.

But it's also worse in its own way. We just checked two items off my list in one night.

* * *

In the morning, after Milo leaves and I shower, I check my email. I squeak when I see Tiffany's name, then click on her note. *Thanks so much for the email. I appreciate your résumé but unfortunately, Brooks & Bailey is going to pass.*

I wince, feeling more ill than I'd have expected from a rejection. Something feels pointed about the words: *We're going to pass.*

That's much different than *we'll let you know* or *if there's a fit, we'll reach out.* TJ is one of their most successful authors. And still, even with a referral, Brooks & Bailey isn't leaving open the door. They're kicking it closed.

They aren't the only ones.

I try to slough off the ick as I get dressed for work, but despite a cute peach dress and my new panties with cat pawprints, my spirits just won't lift.

I feel heavy, weighed down with the sense that time is running out. After I slick on lip gloss, I try on my skull earrings for luck, but I don't feel lucky. They just remind me of the day I was dumb, dumb, dumb.

I take them out, tossing them hard on the vanity. One skids into the toilet. Great. Just great. Now I'm going to dip my fingers in toilet water. Plunging my hand in, I grab the earring, rinse it off, and wash my hands too. But I don't put the earring back in my lobes.

I do not feel lucky, or good, or smart.

What's the lesson now, world?

I've no idea, so I leash up my main squeeze. It's a daycare day, so we head to Throw Me a Bone. Once StudMuffin's settled into the small dog playroom, I leave, pop on shades, and check my email again. First, there's a note from TJ's friend Amelia. *Hey girl! Love your social posts for the flower shop. Love the column. Love everything you do! I'm in London for a show but will write back with more details in a couple days. I have a work idea I want to run past you.*

I respond with a *can't wait*, since what else is there to say? I don't plan to go into the social media business, but maybe social media wants a piece of me.

Possibly, it can fill the gap as I work on my return to books. I wish I were more excited about social media, but maybe I can learn to be excited about it in the same way I am about words and wit.

Then I scroll down and see some new messages.

My breath catches.

Lancaster Abel wrote back quickly. That's my sister's publisher. So did Dunbar Loraine. That's fast too.

I cross my fingers as I walk down the street. *Please let this be good news.*

I click on the Lancaster Abel one first. *Thanks so much for your email. What a delight to hear from one of our top author's family members. So glad you love Hazel's books too. We are thrilled to be publishing them. We will let you know if there are any openings. Many thanks.*

My shoulders sag under the weight of disappointment.

I didn't even warrant an informational interview in the spirit of nepotism. A lump rises rapidly in my throat. A tear slips from one eye, then the other. Blanche may have said nothing, but someone did.

There's no other way I could be this dead to publishing, especially where I have ins like TJ and Hazel.

But I gird myself and click on the Dunbar Loraine note. My last hope.

Dear Veronica,

What a delight to hear from you! We'd love to chat. Can you come by tomorrow at four? If not, we can find another time. Thanks so much,

Alfonso
Editor-At-Large

Oh. My. God.

I'm shaking. I'm so relieved and so happy I'm bouncing in my shoes. I jog the rest of the way to work, googling Alfonso's name. I didn't reach out to him directly, but an editor-at-large inquiry is super promising. When I get to Bikes and Blooms, I unlock the door, then yank it open with a loud clang.

I feel like an ingenue who just stepped off a bus in Hollywood. Hello, world. I'm here.

Milo's bent over, working on a bike before we open.

Trudy's sleeping at his feet. He jerks his gaze to me, then takes off his glasses and sets them in his pocket.

"I have an interview tomorrow!"

His smile takes off for the moon. He's the only one here, so he closes the distance between us in a heartbeat, scoops me up in his arms, and twirls me around. "I knew it! I knew they wouldn't be able to keep their hands off you," he says, his strong, inked arms circling me.

I'm giddy, so jazzed about this chance I'm crying again. But this time, they're tears of relief. Or maybe possibility.

"Thank you. I can't wait. Can you ask Iris to come in?" I ask, swiping my cheek.

He sets me down, tucks a strand of hair over my ear, then drops a kiss to one cheek, then the other, kissing away my tears. "Anything for you," he says, then wraps his arms even tighter around my waist, gazing at me with such tenderness. "I'm excited for you, even though I don't want to let you go."

My breath hitches. Those words thrum through me. They warm my very bones. I know he only means it in relation to work, but a part of me wishes he meant me. Just me.

"I don't even know if I'll get the job," I say, forcing this conversation to stay on the work front. No double meanings need apply.

"You will, and then you'll be gone," he says, wistfully, making it hard for me to stay in the work zone as dangerous thoughts flick through my head.

I don't have to leave you. We could keep doing this. I won't even be working here much longer, regardless.

Then he hums against me, gathering me closer, stroking my hair. "I'll miss seeing you every day," he whispers, and my heart thunders.

My goddess, he's killing me with his sweetness. I want to blurt out my big, blooming feelings for him, tell the man I want more than a list. But he's stated his position—he needs to heal. He's been hurt. I have to respect that.

I smile against him, then steal a glance at the clock. The store opens in ten minutes. Maybe a trip back to the sex zone will do the trick. I'll recalibrate too, on the sex list, and only the list.

"How sturdy is your desk?" I ask.

We find out it's very sturdy, indeed.

24

———

OOPS!

Veronica

The next afternoon at three o'clock, I grab my purse, take a breath, and turn to Iris. "I appreciate you coming in so much," I say.

Despite her tired eyes, she waves it off, then gestures to the flowers. "It's good to be back with my buds," she says, then manages a smile.

I head over to see Milo and Zara, letting them know I'm off for my interview.

"You'll wow them," Zara says, with a note of admiration in her tone.

"She will," Milo says proudly.

I draw a breath of their confidence, then go. On the subway uptown, my phone pings with a text.

Milo: You'll be amazing. I'll meet you outside Central

Park at six-thirty and I fully expect to celebrate.

Veronica: Cross all your fingers and toes.

Milo: Trudy is crossing her paws too.

I'm about to keep this volley going, but I shouldn't rely on him too much. He's not my boyfriend. I can't depend on him, so I click over to another text thread instead—one with my mom and sister.

Veronica: Wish me luck, Valentine ladies.

Mom: You've so got this! Also, I noticed you didn't even ask for outfit approval, which I take as a good sign that you're feeling better about your own radar.

Hazel: She didn't ask me either. Because she knows she's going to kick butt like the Valentine she is!

Veronica: Valentine power!

When the subway rattles into the stop, I turn off my phone, bound to the street, and head inside the Midtown building. After I check in at the lobby, the elevator whisks me upstairs, and quickly, I'm escorted to Alfonso's office.

I've studied the books Alfonso has edited, from celebrity memoirs to a thriller written by a pop star to a children's book penned by an Instagram influencer. He boasts an eclectic list, and I'm eager to hear what he's up to in the kid-lit world.

The dapper man in the checked shirt and smart vest, waiting at the door, smiles. "So pleased to meet you, Miss Valentine. I love your résumé, and your books, and your work," he says, shaking hands, and he's so friendly, I'm halfway in love already.

"So great to meet you too," I say.

He gestures to a chair across from the desk, so I take it and sit while he returns to the desk.

"I enjoyed *March to Your Own Drum*," I add, since I read the instagrammer's book last night.

It wasn't bad.

"Glad to hear that," he says, then goes on to tell me how much he liked *Frog and Prince*. "Your work on that series was tremendous. Agnes was lucky to have you guiding her stories."

I hesitate before I speak. McGee Whitney Books was notoriously cautious about revealing who edited Agnes. She worked with several editors, and usually only spoke broadly about her team. "She's quite a talent," I say, giving a broad answer too.

"She is," Alfonso says, cheerily. Then he clears his throat. "Thank you again for coming in. We are in the early stages of putting together an anthology, and we think you'd be great for it."

I sit up straighter. Fight off a smile. *I would be great.*

"Wonderful. I can't wait to hear about it," I say, eagerly, as shoes click on the hardwood floor outside the office, growing closer. There's a rap on the door. I turn, and it's . . . Darius.

Smiling cloyingly.

"Veronica! My last call ran late, but I'm so glad you could come in. I told Alfonso you'd be perfect for the project."

Darius recommended me? The guy who left McGee Whitney Books because he didn't get the gig? He doesn't seem like the type to refer people.

A warning light flashes on the dashboard, but I steer carefully in case I'm wrong. "Thanks. I appreciate it," I say cautiously.

Darius rubs his palms together. "So are you in?"

Alfonso clears his throat. "I haven't told her the details yet, Mister Daniels."

Darius's smile brightens. "Oh, good. I was worried I missed it," he says, sounding genuinely eager as he strides in and parks himself on the edge of the couch.

Alfonso squares his shoulders. "We're putting together a fun little coffee table book. Stories from various corners of the Web. We're calling it *Oops! Tales from the Internet.*"

My head spins as I begin recalculating this meeting. "I take it this isn't a children's book?"

Darius chortles. "It's so much better, and you'll be perfect," he says.

"No. It's non-fiction," Alfonso continues, exhaling deeply. "Think of it as an anthology. We want to fill it with stories of Internet booboos. Little mistakes and silly do-overs."

The hair on my arms stands on end. "Like Internet humiliations?"

Alfonso snaps his fingers. "Yes, but it's opt in for all the contributors. We're inviting people to tell their own stories. Only if you'd want to share."

Darius gestures to me, a salesman's glint in his eyes. "And you have such a great story to tell. Accidentally sending all of the publishing house the sex column you write. Then, Agnes being haughtier than the Queen. Then McGee Whitney Books trying to cover it up. You could even title your essay . . . The Sex and Sandwich Editor," he says, sweeping out his arm, proud of his title. Then he stage-whispers, "That's how I pitched you."

I feel like I've been slapped. This was a bait and switch. "This meeting isn't about a regular job? It's to ask me to write an essay about the day I lost the job I loved?" I ask, doing my best to keep my cool.

"Yes. We're paying each contributor five hundred dollars," Darius adds, oblivious to my discomfort. But then, he was always oblivious to feelings that weren't his own.

Alfonso offers a kind smile my way. At least he can read a room. "Well, we think you could write it with such cheek, since, well . . ."

Since I write sex columns.

But I keep that to myself. I don't need to throw a hissy fit in front of Alfonso.

Even though I want to ask what he thinks of the fact

that his new employee broke the NDA, since Darius clearly spilled the beans.

But why?

"I'll be the editor, and we think your piece would be a great lead essay," Darius adds.

There it is. His reason. The simplest one of all. He's perched eagerly on the edge of the couch because he thought my shame would help him. He shared my name, he told my story, because he wants a leg up on his project.

I can't truly be mad at him. I'm the one who hit send that night more than a month ago. I can't even blame the cat.

But I also don't have to stay here.

I lift my chin. Nothing to hide. "Thank you, but I'm trying to move on from that day." Then I turn to Alfonso. "If you have any jobs in children's books, do let me know."

"Of course. Thank you, Miss Valentine," he says, studying the floor like it's so very interesting as he shows me out.

As I wait at the elevator, gritting my teeth, reining in my hurt, Darius catches up to me. "What's the deal, Veronica? I don't even get a thank you? I was doing you a favor."

"Excuse me?" I ask, shocked. "You want me to thank you? Because you broke an NDA?"

He shrugs carelessly. "It was unenforceable once I left. What were they going to do? Fire me after I quit?" he asks, scoffing and revealing the flimsiness of the NDA. Quite clearly, he's told everyone in publishing the tale of my humiliation. "Besides, that stuff never stays quiet anyway. At least I'm trying to get you something out of it. C'mon. This is going to be a marquee project," he says, making his last pitch. "We need a killer lead essay, and I figured you'd need the money. Since you don't have a real job," he says.

I seethe privately, but then tamp down my emotions, and put on a smile. People who make me feel small don't deserve my time or my heartache.

I won't stoop to his mercenary level though. The world is small and reputations can crumble at any moment. "Thank you, Darius. But I do have a job. I'm much happier selling flowers and writing about sex toys and fantasies."

That's true.

That's completely, absolutely true.

Even though one of those jobs will be ending in a few more weeks. As I leave, I purse my lips, holding back my tears.

I don't let a single one slip until I'm at least a block away.

25

———

ACE IN MY HOLE

Milo

When I see Veronica outside Central Park, sitting on a bench, reading on her phone, my first instinct is to wrap her up in my arms. Then tell her Dunbar Loraine are a bunch of jerks. That they don't deserve her. I still can't believe they tricked her like that.

As I walk closer, her shoulders tremble. She bites her lip, like she's fighting off tears. She dabs at her cheek with a tissue.

My heart squeezes painfully.

She takes a breath, swipes on the screen, and keeps reading. She's trying to be so strong. "Hey, sunshine," I say softly when I reach her.

Startled, she looks up. She knew I was coming to meet her, but the second I got her text that the interview was a bust, I came early, leaving Zara and Iris to close the store.

Veronica flashes me a sad smile. "Hi."

I sit next to her on the bench and wrap an arm around her. "I'm sorry it didn't work out," I say into her soft hair.

"Me too." Her voice wobbles. But then she takes a breath. "But it's fine. I'm fine." She separates from me, smooths her skirt, and drapes on a smile. "We can still get a drink and try that thing from the list."

Oh, hell no. "Veronica, you don't have to put on a brave face for me."

"But I want to do number four," she says, imploring, and I believe her but in the broad sense, not the *right now* sense.

I reach for her hand, lock my fingers with hers. "Look, sex is the ultimate feel-good drug. And I want to do so many damn things with you," I say, resisting the urge to admit that this list of five is nowhere near enough. I want ten, twenty, thirty to-do items with her. Hell, make that one hundred. "But let me take you out tonight. Let's just wander around the park like we planned." But I have a better idea. Something more fun —that's what she needs right now. "Or . . . we could go to check out some rooftop gardens in Brooklyn. Go to some super-hip too-cool-for-school restaurant and people watch and make up stories. Then stop at a lingerie shop and buy you more of your crazy undies. Like a sexy bikini barely-there number with unicorns on it," I say, wiggling my brows as I picture her sweet ass in a new pair of cheeky undies.

Now, she's smiling for real. Laughing too. I drink in

that look on her face, knowing I put it there, and I want to do that again and again.

"That sounds like fun, Mister Good Times," she says.

"That's me, and you need fun," I say, and I wish I could offer her a true solution. Like a job. "I would hire you, Veronica. I mean it. I would hire you full-time. You're the best thing to happen to the store." I bring my finger to my lips. "Don't tell Iris, but you're the real star."

She scoffs, all faux bashful. "Stahp, stahp."

But she's still grinning, and I can't help myself. I take both her hands in mine and pull her close. "You're the secret sauce. The magic bullet. You're . . . my ace in the hole."

"You want to put your ace in my hole," she says with a wiggle of her brows.

"That's my woman."

Her expression falters at those words.

Shit. I called her *my woman*. But she does feel like my woman, and I don't know what the hell to do about that.

Veronica Valentine is wreaking havoc with my heart. I want to be the man to help her through these tough times. To solve this problem for her. "I know there's a big world out there and so many things you can do. I could easily rattle off ten, twenty jobs for you. You're so lively and clever, and you have such a big brain and heart," I say.

She shakes her head, gently calling off my attempt to be helpful. "I don't want to talk about work anymore. Can we just go . . . have fun?"

"Absolutely."

I order a Lyft, and we spend the next few hours checking out rooftop gardens in Brooklyn, an herb shop, a crepe truck, and a stationery store where she buys new gel pens. When we're done, she makes her way to the nearest subway station.

I shudder, grabbing her hand to stop her before she descends those dirty stairs. "I hate subways," I say.

"Why? You don't want to get your pretty clothes dirty?"

I nod. "Yes. That. Right there. Also, I don't like rats, or poles that thousands of people touch, and well, crowds."

"Fair enough," she says with a laugh. "You're seriously cute."

We take a Lyft back to Grove Street. When the car drops us off, neither of us asks where we're spending the night. We just grab our dogs, go for a walk, and wind up back at her place.

But we don't tackle an item on her extra list—sixty-nine.

Instead, when we get into bed, I bring her into an embrace under the covers.

"Milo," she whispers, sounding concerned.

"Yes?"

"I'm not broken. Even though I had a bad day, I still want your dick."

I laugh. "Have I mentioned I love your crassness?"

"A few times," she says. She heaves a sigh, then stares at me in the dark, her gaze inquisitive. "But is there a reason you're not trying to get me naked?"

She caught me, and I like it. Now I have to admit it,

but Veronica makes sharing my heart easier than I'd expected.

"I think I just wanted to make sure I was giving you everything you needed in other ways first," I confess, even if it gives away how much I care.

She leans closer, presses a firm kiss to my lips. "You are. Now, please, get the hell inside me."

And the truth was worth it.

A few minutes later, we're naked and breathless. She's under me, legs wrapped tightly around me, her fingers gripping my ass.

She holds on tight as I swivel my hips.

A gorgeous shudder moves down her body as I quicken the pace. Her hands slide up my back, her fingers playing with my hair.

I meet her eyes. Those green irises are so full of passion, lust and, a fiery new thing—true emotion.

And I know, as the pleasure tips over in me, that I'm so close to losing my heart.

Or maybe I already have.

And after a few more minutes, the world winks off, and we come together.

* * *

A little later, I'm yawning, ready to conk out, when I spot a paperback on her nightstand. I can't make out the cover, but that's not the point. "What if you wrote your columns into a book? I bet someone would publish that," I ask in the dark, feeling a little brilliant. I've been wanting to find a solution for her work problems—something that suits her shiny, sexy mind.

She ruffles my hair. "Maybe, but I don't know if that's a living. Though I'm pretty sure I'll need to write about you plucking my petal soon in my column. Do you mind, Mister Sexy Pants?"

I yawn again, shaking my head. "Hell no. I want all your readers to know I'm the one who got you," I say.

I do want to be the one to keep her. The only one. And that wish is so much trouble for my damaged heart.

26

BALCONY GARDENER

Veronica

Last night with Milo was the medicine I needed. He tapped my funny bone *and* my ass.

But more than that—the man lifted my spirits.

Now, as I get dressed in the morning, with Milo finishing his coffee in the kitchen after taking the early dog-walking shift, I feel refreshed. Ready to tackle the terrifying unknown of the big J-O-B search.

Wallowing is no longer an option, even as all of kid-lit slams its doors on me. I won't mourn. I will move on.

Because I've learned that taking charge rocks. In this last week with Milo, I've taken charge of my pleasure, and I've reaped the rewards.

I'll lady-boss my career too.

With the morning sun illuminating my closet, I spot my infamous red polka-dot skirt, and it's calling my name. I wore this the afternoon Milo and I nearly crashed into each other. That day upended my life and sent me down the path to his shop. I didn't think I'd like selling flowers so much. But turns out, I'm damn good at chatting with customers, recommending the right blooms, then coming up with fun marketing slogans.

Am I ready to be the bawdy florist? Or maybe something similar? While I hunt for the next big thing, perhaps I'll do social media to pay the bills or try my hand at freelance editing.

I picture the pages of the fireman calendar in my kitchen flipping by in a blur. My job ends in less than six weeks. But since Milo is going out of town today, I'll devote all of tonight and tomorrow to the search. I tug on the skirt, grab my skull earrings from the top of the bureau, and pop them in.

I leave my bedroom and *whoa.*

Milo's in my kitchen, twisting a tiny tool thingamajig into a loose hinge on a cabinet. His pale-yellow shirt rides up, displaying a sliver of his flat stomach.

I hum low in my throat as I come into the room. "Some women fantasize about waking up to find a hot man making her pancakes and bacon. I fantasize about walking in on a hot guy working his tools."

"Better not be just any hot guy," he tosses out.

"Oh, it's definitely you," I say.

He cranes his neck, then flashes a big, sexy smile. "I know, sunshine. Like I said, I memorized all your columns, including the one where you wanted me to fix a broken pipe," he says, making me warm and fuzzy. "Maybe that's why I carry a Leatherman in my pocket."

"And all this time I just thought you were happy to see me."

He laughs. "We're both happy to see you."

He returns to the fix-it job, and I return to ogling. What a view. What a man.

My career might be a mystery novel, but my dating life doesn't need a detective. If I had to pen a *Virgin Club* column today, I'd say *find the person who fixes your broken cabinet, kisses your tears, and lifts your spirits. Also, ideally, the one who fucks you just the way you want.*

As I drink him in, my heart writes the next sentence. *And then keep him.*

Perhaps, it's time to take charge of my heart too. Sure, there's that little trouble of Milo's dating hiatus. But we don't have to dive in over our heads. Would he be willing to wade into the shallow end with me?

I fidget with my earring, twisting it around.

I could try. I could ask him out on a real date. Something beyond *let's grab grub before we bang.*

My palms sweat. I swipe them on my skirt as he pats the sturdy hinge, closes the cupboard, then drops the Leatherman in his pocket.

He crosses the distance in the small kitchen, looks me up and down. His gaze flips my insides. "You doing better today?"

"I am. Thanks again for last night."

I practice in my head: *Thank you for showing me your heart, and can I please keep it for myself?*

"Anytime. And don't think you're getting out of the final item on your list," he says.

"I wouldn't dream of it," I say, silently adding *we can*

be more than a top-five list.

"Mmm. Love that list," he says, then gently brings me in for a kiss. My toes flutter. If I were writing a column just for him, I'd want to reassure him with: *I know you're scared of relationships, but I won't hurt you. I just want to be yours and you can be mine.*

When we break the kiss, he says, "I leave tonight for the bike ride. But I'll be back at work on Tuesday. We can tackle the rest of the list then if you want. I can give you the code to my home, and you can come find me in the shower," he adds, his voice low and dirty.

He's still focused on sex, which is understandable. I need to ease him into the idea that we level up to romance.

I glance toward the living room, where the dogs are sharing a giraffe toy, and on to the balcony, with its garden of small pots.

That's what I need to do—plant the seeds of a possible romance. I turn back to Milo. "What if we get dinner too? And maybe we could extend the list," I say.

His lips curve up. "Miss Cute Devil Butt has some more fantasies?"

"I do." *Of you and me together for real.* The list can be a springboard, and on Tuesday, I'll spell out my heart.

"So, we keep going?" He sounds intrigued.

I'm breathless with hope, and I want him to see how easy romance with me can be. "I want to. Do you? I mean, right now we work together and it's complicated, but in another month, there won't even be any potential awkwardness at work with other employees wondering what's up. Or anything like that," I add.

His expression goes blank for a few seconds, like he forgot something, then he blows out a breath. "Ah, shit. Somewhere along the way, I think I stopped worrying about that," he says, wincing, like this reawakened thought pains him. "But maybe, I probably should worry about it more. I don't want my dating life to drag things down at Bikes and Blooms."

I shirk back. "I would never leave a bad review," I say, a little offended.

Quickly, he shakes his head. "Oh no, I didn't mean that. I just meant I should probably do a better job keeping everything separate. I don't want one to affect the other."

I relax a bit. But only a bit. "Sure. That makes sense. You have to think about Zara and Ian and Iris and James."

"Exactly. And customers. I don't want my personal life causing problems for the business," he says with a frown.

I'm not a troublemaker, I want to shout.

Except, there is probably more to his careless words. They might mask a real issue.

A warning light blinks in my mind, telling me to slow down. Maybe even to hit pause on my ask-him-out plan. Because . . . is his tapping the brakes a sign he's just not ready? If so, there's nothing I can do to make him ready.

But when Trudy rises and stretches her front legs, that's a clear sign the time has run out for us this morning.

"Bryan's meeting me at my place in a few minutes to

pick her up, but I'll see you at work soon. Should be a busy day," he says, then, like he's swiping away his worries, his expression clears and he drops a kiss to my forehead. "And the answer is . . . yes."

I smile softly, but I don't feel his *yes* in my bones or my heart.

Milo and Trudy take off, and when the door snaps closed, Hot Stuff sashays across the kitchen counter, shooting me a look of disapproval.

He walks on by, tail held high, as if saying *you chickened out.*

Maybe he's right.

But maybe it was necessary.

On the way to work, I shove romance out of my mind. Time to focus on the next big thing. I'll start now, reaching out to Jessica at Little Artists to get the ball rolling on social media.

As I walk, I click on my inbox to send her a note, but before I can draft one, I spot an email from TJ's friend Amelia, the lead singer for Ten-Speed Rabbit. She's asking me to meet for coffee tomorrow.

Then she tells me about her proposal, and I see her vision from her description. It's sexy and quirky and right on brand.

I gasp, stopping in the middle of the sidewalk, realizing I'm seeing *my* vision.

I see my next big thing. Looks like the detective cracked the mystery of her career.

27

THE MOTHER OF ALL
COMPLICATIONS

Milo

Where the hell is Trudy's measuring cup? I yank open a drawer, hunting for it in my kitchen. It should be here with the utensils.

But it's not.

I jerk open another one, irritated I can't find it. Ah, there it is. "She gets this much food in the morning," I say, waggling the three-quarter measuring cup at my brother.

Bryan snorts. "You think I'm going to feed this queen mere dog food? No way. I'll be cooking steak for Trudy."

I shoot him a *don't-you-dare* look. "It'll make her tummy hurt."

He snort-laughs. "Did you really just say *tummy*?"

"Are you mocking me for how I talk about the love

of my life?" I ask as I grab a small Tupperware container of organic dog food.

My big brother crosses his big arms over his big chest. "I am," he says, with a satisfied grin. "Listen to yourself."

"She's a devoted dog. She doesn't double cross me," I say, a little less flustered, but not by much. Why the hell am I so antsy this morning? Just because I'm leaving town for a bike ride?

"But can she stay up late? What's her curfew?"

I roll my eyes, but I'm too rattled to take the bait. I rush into the living room to grab a stuffed monkey from the basket, then jam the toy into a backpack for Trudy. Maybe she's also why I'm jittery. This is the first time I'm leaving her since I've had her back. What if Callie reappears and tries to steal her? But that's silly. Callie couldn't wrestle the dog away from my brother, or me. And we signed the custody paperwork.

Besides, I'll probably never see Callie again.

I do my best to shake off the stress as I stride over to Bryan, who's leaning against the kitchen wall. "Seriously, I'm glad she's staying with you. This whole bike ride is last minute, so I appreciate you watching her."

My brother slugs my arm. "Anytime. Though not for much longer," he says, a little wistfully.

I pout. "Don't remind me you're leaving for Los Angeles. I can't handle too much change," I say, then I drop Trudy's food into the backpack and grab my own bag, and we head out of my place.

With Trudy leading the way, we walk down Grove Street. Even though Veronica likely left her home already, I can't help but look at her balcony. My heart tugs, almost painfully, but like it's pointing at the answer.

Oh, hell.

That's it. That convo with Veronica did me in. I can't believe I've been so caught up in her that I barely thought about how all these feelings for her might affect my business.

I wasn't paying attention at all to the shop.

I've been so distracted by the amazing sex and the awesome conversation and the incredible woman that I haven't even thought once about the consequences at Bikes and Blooms.

Will we ruin the vibe at the store with Zara and Ian and James and Iris *and* customers if we keep canoodling for the next few weeks?

It's a risk.

But I'll also miss Veronica while I'm gone the next two days. That realization makes me jittery too. I stare at her deck longer than I should.

"Is that your friend's place?" Bryan asks, catching on.

No point denying it. "Yeah. That's Veronica's home," I admit, snapping my gaze back to my brother.

"Ah, Miss Yoga Pants," he says.

I laugh, remembering that name I gave her once upon a time. "Kind of funny one of my nicknames for her was Miss Yoga Pants and hers for me was Mister Sexy Pants."

"Oh man, do you hear that dopey grin sound in your voice?" he asks with a chuckle. "You sound ass over elbow, like it was all meant to be."

I jerk my gaze to him, hackles raised. "I do?"

"Yeah, you do."

My pulse skyrockets, too high, too fast. Last night, I sensed my feelings for her were shooting to the sky. If my brother can spot them this easily, I could be in too deep before I'm ready.

Am I ready?

I don't even know. But when I think with my heart instead of my head, I make bad decisions. I ignore my radar. Hell, my compass is probably irreparably broken.

"Fuck," I mutter as we walk past a loud bus, its exhaust spewing stinky air at my face. "What am I supposed to do?"

"What do you *want* to do?" Bryan asks in his low-key style. I got all the strung-too-tight genes.

Shoving a hand through my hair, I try to sort through the mess in my head. "I want to ask her out for real. I'm kind of crazy for her. But I don't trust anyone, and dating is toxic, and we work together, *and* I've only just gotten out of that five grand hole. And . . . *fuck.*"

He sets a reassuring hand on my shoulder as we walk. "You're hyperventilating, Milo." He's a gentle giant, and I'm a wound-up jack-in-the-box.

Deep breath.

"What do I do?" I ask, but my stupid voice is pitching up, up, up.

"Slow down. Breathe," he says.

I take another big gulp of hot, sticky summer air, chased by bus fumes.

Not helping, New York.

I glance at my pup, trotting gamely ahead of me

without a care in the world.

I can't swing through life carefree, like I've done for the last week with Veronica. I'm not a dog. I'm a man with a fledgling business, and employees, and a reputation I'm rebuilding.

When we reach Seventh Avenue, I hug Trudy then hand Bryan the leash. "Thanks again."

He yanks me in for an embrace. "Try to unwind when you're on your ride. Maybe you just need a few days to clear your head."

It's probably good advice, but when I get to work, Zara tells me the bike blogger called and wants his new wheels two days early.

As in . . . today.

I put on my glasses and get to work.

* * *

A few hours later, I'm this close to finishing the custom build for Rio, the bike blogger. He's coming in an hour. Once he tests the bike, I should be able to take off.

As I'm threading the chain in the back of the shop, my phone trills with Iris's ringtone.

Weird. She rarely calls. She's a classic texter. With the chain locked in, I wipe my hand on a rag in time to answer. "Hey mama, what's cooking?"

As I step into the doorway of the shop, checking out the bikes and the blooms, Iris sighs heavily. "Milo, I'm sorry to do this but yesterday was so hard for me."

My brow knits. "What do you mean?"

"I missed Danny too much," she says, her voice trembling. "I don't think I'm ready to come back to work."

I grab the wall of the shop to steady myself. "You . . . don't want to return?" I ask, as Veronica swings her gaze to me from the counter where she's working.

"I wanted to give you as much notice as possible," Iris continues. "But I don't think I can come back full-time. I only want to work on Saturdays."

Iris has been so passionate about the shop since I started it. I never thought she'd drop to part-time. Now I'll have to hunt for a replacement

Again.

Ohhh. Duh.

The answer to Veronica's temporary work need is staring at me.

The answer to *mine* is staring at me too.

"I totally understand, Iris," I say, then after we finish the details and I hang up, Veronica shoots me a sympathetic look. "She isn't ready to come back?"

I nod weakly, still reeling a bit from the surprise. "I should have seen this coming. But I didn't. That seems to be the theme for today," I admit with a shrug. I glance toward the door, then at the chalkboard sign beyond, then back to the woman I adore. I already mixed business with pleasure into a giant soup of feelings and fear. At this point, what kind of schmuck would I be not to offer her the gig? "You're the best thing to ever happen to the blooms in Bikes and Blooms. Do you want to stay until . . . you figure out your next move?"

"I would but—"

The door swings open and the mother of all complications walks in.

28

CALL IT GOOD

Milo

What does she want now? My head swims with new worries as Callie strides toward me like she owns the flooring, the ceiling, and all the shelves, flowers, and bikes.

This woman should be required to carry a whip to warn others what she's like.

Instead, she's full con artist, decked out in costume so damn innocently—pink Converse sneakers, khaki shorts, and a tank top. When she reaches me in the middle of the flower shop, she flashes a megawatt smile.

This is the only time I'm grateful for a lull in foot traffic. There are no customers shopping for buds. But Zara looks up from the bike counter, then walks around it, flanking me like a bodyguard.

Callie tilts her head, her eyes sweeping my face. "Milo, sweetheart. You have grease on your cheek. I swear, you're such a cute, hot mess. Last time it was glitter. Let me help you," she says, lifting a hand.

Flinching, I step away. "What do you want?" I bite out.

She pouts. "Is that any way to greet one of your business partners?"

"Excuse me?"

Smoothly, she gestures toward the shop in the back, where the wheels for Rio's ride are visible through the open door. "I follow you online, and I'm so excited to see your custom bike business is growing. It's thrilling."

Zara crosses her arms. "Because Milo works hard at it," she growls.

Callie's smile ripens. "Hard work is so important, and so are ideas," she says, then sighs, a long, horrifyingly self-satisfied one. "Like how I gave you the idea for the custom bike business."

Red billows from my eyes. Are you kidding me? "You did not give me the idea," I hiss.

"Didn't I, though? Weren't you talking about how to expand, and I mentioned the shop in Williamsburg was all the rage with its custom bikes? And you should try your hand at custom bikes? I said it one night when we were walking *Baby*."

That. Name.

It's a miracle I don't blow a fuse right now. Inside, all my circuits are breaking. "It's not an original fucking idea. It's a normal thing."

"It's *the* thing in the specialized bike biz," Zara adds.

Callie bobs a shoulder. "If you say so, but if you're going to be difficult about sharing the profits, Milo, I can just have my attorney handle this. He'll be in touch," she says, then spins on her sneakered feet and walks out in a cloud of perfume and trickery.

When the door slams shut, Zara closes the distance and cups my shoulders. "She's trying to scare you," Zara says, calm and reassuring. "Don't let her."

I grit my teeth. "I won't," I bite out.

But Callie's plan is working. I *am* fucking scared.

I turn my gaze to Veronica, who's busying herself spraying the flowers with water.

Veronica came up with so many new ideas for my flower business.

She's not like Callie. Not one bit. I know that in my heart, and yet, I have no good instincts. I trusted Callie enough to move in with her, to share a home with her, to fall for her.

"Excuse me," I say, and I leave, then walk around the block, once, twice, three times, trying to chase the onslaught of terrible thoughts away.

When I return, the clock ticking perilously close to Rio's pickup time, I zoom in on work. I finish the job with blinders on. As I'm polishing the handlebars and chewing on my own stupidity, Veronica comes over to me, a soft, sympathetic look in her eyes. "Is it easier for you if we just . . . call it good? With the list?"

No. Hell no.

And yet, some of my tension seeps away at the question. "You sure?"

She nods. "It's been fun, but it sounds like you should just focus on your business right now."

She's so earnest. So real. And I am so in love with

her that I don't trust myself not to fuck up everything I've built.

"That's probably a good idea," I say, right as Rio comes in.

I turn away from Veronica, stride up to him, shake his hand. "It's all ready."

He's all smiles. "I knew I could count on you," he says.

That makes only one of us.

29

THE MAN BLUES

Veronica

Fine, I do wallow.

But this time it's not over a job. It's over a man, and hey, that's allowed.

That night, Ellie drags my ass to Gin Joint to meet Hazel and indulge in the *amazing new summer-themed mojitos* the bar is offering.

"They're the perfect cure for the man blues," Ellie says as we turn on the corner, heading toward the popular speakeasy in Chelsea. "Trust me. Sebastian and I were talking about this on set."

"Dude. Did you just name drop an Oscar winner?"

Ellie winces. "Shit. I did. I'm an asshole."

I laugh. "No, you're not. I suppose if I worked with him, I'd do the same."

"He's such a sweetheart, and besides, the mojitos

worked for both of us, and they are going to work for you," she says, chin up and best friend-y.

I need something to lift my spirits after that *I volunteer as tribute* stunt I pulled at the store this afternoon.

Ugh. "What was I thinking?" I ask as we reach the bar.

"You did the noble thing," Ellie says, and I trudge into the establishment with her.

"I'm still waiting for my knighting," I say, listless and sad.

As soon as we're through the door, Hazel pops up from a sapphire chaise longue, marches over to me, and wraps me in her big-sister arms. I sniffle a little as she hugs me, but then I let go, determined to put today behind me.

"Are you okay?" Hazel asks, hands curled around my shoulders, green eyes pinning me.

I haul in a deep breath as the chatter of the bar fills my head—glasses clinking, conversations unspooling, laughter bursting. "I'll be fine," I say, fastening on a stiff upper lip. Really, what did I have to mourn anyway? The end of a sex countdown? I'll get over it. I have to. "It was no big deal."

Hazel taps my nose. "Did that just grow, Pinocchio?"

"But it *has* to be no big deal. He's my boss for a while longer, but even if I didn't work for him, he's just not emotionally available and there's nothing I can do about—"

A dapper lounge singer at the baby grand dives into the opening notes of an unfamiliar love song. It's old-fashioned and beautiful as he croons in a rich, plaintive voice, *Let me call you sweetheart. I'm in love with you. Let me hear you whisper. That you love me too.*

My heart swells like a balloon, then pops. All the air leaks out, and my chest aches. My throat hurts. I turn to Hazel and whisper past the stranglehold this song has on me. "I need to go."

* * *

Thirty minutes later, I've claimed a booth with Ellie and Hazel at a classic New York diner with cracked upholstery, orange Formica, and milkshakes and fries all around.

It's the official menu of the sad. I sigh again, stirring the thick chocolatey goodness. "I just thought that we were about to become something. Milo seemed so . . ." I stop, search for the words as I meet their twin gazes.

"Real," I say, nearly choking on the word. "I had all these fantasies about him, and then I met him, and he seemed so real."

Hazel stretches out a hand and squeezes mine. "He sounds great."

I appreciate that they're not demonizing him, but . . .

"I feel pretty foolish even though he never fooled me. He was honest from the start. I just wanted more, but when I saw him struggling this afternoon, I wanted to give him an out."

"Maybe someday he'll see what's in front of him. But for now, you're going to keep on moving, right?" Ellie asks, lifting her silver shaker. "We can't let men get the better of us."

"I couldn't agree more," I say, raising a glass too.

Hazel lifts her shake. "Hear, hear."

As we toast, I feel strong for the first time since this afternoon. I feel confident again. "I think I know exactly how I'll keep on moving," I whisper, excited once again for tomorrow as I share my plan.

The next morning, I head into Big Cup early for my meeting with Amelia.

I scan the shop, picking a table in advance since she's not here yet, then head to the counter. Instantly, I grin when I see the blue-eyed, fresh-faced barista. "Anna! It's been a while. How are you?"

The pretty blonde flashes a grin. "I can't complain. How are you? I've been following your recent columns," she says, then leans in close. "And getting some ideas myself."

Anna's a friend and one of my first readers. I even showed her one of my early columns for feedback. She fell in love with *The Virgin Club* from the start and has kept tabs on it since then.

"Then the column is doing its job," I say. *And fingers crossed that it might keep doing so in a very big way in, oh, say, five minutes.*

"Your recommendations definitely keep me busy. From one woman with a dirty mind to another," Anna adds.

There's only one little issue. "Well, I'm going to have to turn in my card," I admit, but today I don't feel as sad about the Milo situation as I did last night.

Anna's eyes widen. "Will we get the details?"

That's a good question. I'll figure out the answer soon enough.

"Maybe," I say with a coy shrug. "But woman to woman, I'll tell you this—it was worth the wait."

Anna sighs happily.

Milo was worth the wait. I chose wisely. I have no regrets.

I place my coffee order, then ask what she's been up to as she makes the drink.

"I was in Paris, visiting the shop there. I might need to go there full-time. Family obligations and all. But if you ever need a guest columnist, I have lots of ideas I've been wanting to explore," she says.

"Thanks. I'll let The Dating Pool know," I say, then I take my coffee and head to a table.

A minute later, a gorgeous Amelia bursts in, all mad energy and little red dress. As she surveys the shop, I pop up.

She rushes over to me. "You! You, goddess, you! You are just the person I need for my show," she continues. "But I need a cuppa first." The British singer sails off to the counter and orders an Earl Grey.

When she returns, she sits down in a cloud of shampoo-model curls, cheekbones, and sex appeal. "Here's the deal. I have a concert here in a month. And a new song called "Battery-Operated Friend" to debut. I want to include gift bags with every ticket—a hand-curated package of sex toys. And you're just the one to pick them."

I sit up straighter, enjoying stepping into the next big thing. "I am indeed just the one."

30

LADY TROUBLE

Milo

I wiggle around on the uncomfortable earth as crickets chirp outside the tent.

"This sleeping bag sucks," I grumble, jerking the nylon contraption closer to the edge of the tent, away from this stupid leaf under me. Or acorn. Or pit in the center of the earth that will swallow me whole.

From the other side of the tent, Drew clears his throat, then calls out softly, "Axel, you got that? Is that Milo's fiftieth or fifty-first complaint about something today?"

Axel hums in the dark of the Hudson Valley on Sunday night after a long, exhausting day of riding through the hills. "Let's see. Forty-nine was his bike pants were cutting off circulation to his brain. Fifty was the bike seat making his dick hurt. Yup. Sleeping bag makes fifty-one. Good job counting, Drew."

"I did not say the pants cut off circulation to my brain," I hiss.

Drew waves a hand. "Brain. Balls. Same thing with you, Goldilocks."

I heave a sigh. "But the sleeping bag does suck. I can feel every damn lump in the ground," I mutter as I kick the end of the bag.

"Aww, want me to get you a Serta mattress next time?" Drew teases.

"I doubt you're comfortable either. This is the world's smallest three-person tent," I point out.

"There would be more room if you slept outside the tent, Milo," Axel deadpans. "Maybe consider that."

I roll my eyes, even though these fuckers can't see me in the dark. "There would be more room if Drew didn't crash the ride at the last minute," I point out, because I'm an asshole.

"Dude, did you or did you not in-fucking-vite me? I had a break after training camp and I came back here at your request, dickhead," he snaps.

Shit. I am a bad friend. I am a bad boss. I am a bad everything.

"I'm sorry, man," I say, meaning it. "I didn't mean to take it out on you. I'm just a mess."

"There, there," Axel says drily, patting the ground next to me. "Everything is forgiven when you have lady trouble."

Hold on. How did he know? I jerk my gaze toward him. "Was it that obvious?"

The two of them snort in unison.

"Um, yeah," Drew says.

"Like an open fucking book," Axel adds.

I should just go to sleep. I should just shut up. I should just curl up and forget yesterday. But I miss Veronica insanely. I don't know what to do about *calling it good*. I don't want to call it good. I want to call her up and see her every damn day and night. Then there's the matter of Callie. I shudder. Sitting, I scrub a hand over my jaw. "I need help. I need a lawyer again for starters," I say, embarrassed my life has come to this.

Drew and Axel sit up too. With the shadows playing on their faces, I can see both their expressions shift to serious in the moonlight.

"What's going on, man? Is this why you've been riding like there's a hornet's nest in your pants?" Drew asks, no teasing now.

"Callie threatened me," I confess, then I tell them what she said when she showed up.

Axel shakes his head, huffing out an annoyed breath. "Why didn't you tell me sooner? I did go to law school."

"I guess I wanted to just ignore it. Also, you don't practice stupid shit law," I say.

He laughs. "I don't practice at all, but I took the bar and I understand the law. This is spurious. We'll send her a letter. I'll sign it with my legal name."

I snort out a laugh. "Don't want her connecting the dots with my lawyer, Alexander Hendrix-Blythe, and the thriller writer, Axel Huxley."

"And I'll add the fancy esquire too. That always freaks people out," he adds.

Drew shivers. "The *esquire* is terrifying."

"I second that," I say.

"But don't let her threats get to you," Axel reassures me. "You can't patent a custom bike shop idea any more than you can patent a bike and flower shop concept."

I breathe easily for the first time in more than a day. "Thanks, man. I should have brought it up sooner instead of stewing. I can't even tell you how much I appreciate that."

"No problem." Axel takes a beat. "But I would still have more room if you slept outside the tent."

Drew clears his throat. "I would too."

"Oh, fuck off," I say, but I'm laughing now too.

"Hey, we put up with your shit mood for the last day. So, now, 'fess up. What's the lady trouble?" Drew asks.

I only scratched the surface there, so I dig deeper and tell my buds about the real hurt in my heart, finishing with, "And then she said we should call it good. So, maybe she didn't want to finish the list, or see me on Tuesday. Which sucks, since I fell in love with her, but—"

"—No. Just no," Drew snaps.

"No what?" I ask, confused.

"Whatever you're going to say is wrong. You fell in love with her and she offered to fall on the sword. *For you*. You don't get to turn that around."

Damn. The dude's intense with his love advice. "But wasn't she kind of saying she wanted to end things?"

Axel smacks his palm against the ground. "Man, Callie did a number on you," he says, in between laughs. "You are such a numb nut."

I am. And I was the biggest one yesterday. Realization dawns fully as I replay the conversation in the shop one more time. *Is it easier for you if we just . . . call it good?* Veronica sacrificed us for me. "Veronica's the anti-Callie. She did *that* for *me*. Oh, shit. I am a whole box of numb nuts."

Axel holds out his arms, like *I told you so.*

Drew smiles wickedly. "This was officially worth flying across the country to hear."

I spend the next day riding my ass off and figuring out how to fix my mistake.

31

A BUSY BEAVER

Veronica

I am the busiest beaver in New York City on Sunday night. I'm having drinks with the women from Just for Her at The Lucky Spot.

I contacted Angelica, Lark, and Christine the second I left the café with Amelia this morning. They're local, so they offered to meet right away.

"We would love to help you put the gift bag together with some of our gifties," Lark says as our drinks arrive, and she thanks the server.

"Now, what are your faves?" Angelica asks, lifting her martini for a sip.

I reach for my iced tea and drink too, then rattle off some of my favorites. "The Butterfly of course. That's just so . . ." I wriggle a little bit in my chair. "Cha cha cha," I say in a sultry tone.

Lark laughs, a smoky, sexy sound. "It makes me want to do the samba too."

"But I also love The Wave, and for women who've struggled to orgasm, it's life-changing," I say.

"Everyone should have orgasms," Angelica says plainly.

"I couldn't agree more," I say, and we chat further about the life-changing magic of regular climaxes.

Yes, I am with my people, just like I am when I talk to readers at The Dating Pool.

We wrap the meeting, and as soon as I leave the bar, I call Bellamy and tell her I'd love to make the Q and A into a regular thing and use it to launch my new business idea. She says yes immediately, and I am bouncing.

There's only one more person I need to talk to.

Early Monday morning, I race to Midtown at eight-thirty and pop into Doctor Insomnia's Tea and Coffee Emporium to grab coffee with my former boss. "So this might sound wild," I say, diving into the deep end. "I want to start a date-night subscription box. and I think I could be really good at it. But, here's the twist."

Blanche's eyebrows lift in anticipation. "I love a good twist."

"I want to call it Date Night for One. Have a date night with yourself. Curated by me—the erstwhile friendly neighborhood virgin turned sex-for-one expert. It'll include my favorite picks for sex toys, little write-ups about each one, and how and why they work best, as well as cute little notebooks and pens for writing down your fantasies. It'll be all about self-care. But the best kind of self-care there is," I say with a naughty grin.

"Orgasm care," Blanche supplies. "I love it. How can I help?"

"I would love your advice on how to grow this new business. I have a chance to launch it at a Ten-Speed Rabbit concert, and I want to go bigger. You said you have a mentorship group, so I would be grateful for any insight on finding loans and so on to get started."

Blanche's bright blue eyes twinkle. "I could definitely give you some advice. And . . ." She taps her nails on the table, like she's thinking. "I could also provide the initial funding. I'd like to."

My. Head. Explodes.

My former boss wants to invest in my new business?

"You would?" I ask, stammering.

"Actually, let me revise that. I'd love to invest," she says. "This is women helping women. It's all about female desire. You made me a brand-new sexual person, and I'd like to help you become an entrepreneur."

I sit back in my chair, soaking in her offer. "You're a fairy godmother."

She mimes waving a magic wand. "You get an O, and you get an O, and you get an O."

"Bibbidi-Bobbidi-Boo."

* * *

That evening, I'm pacing my balcony, debating ideas for my next column. But I'm stuck.

And I think I know why. I've always been honest with my readers about my desires. Hell, I encourage them to be honest about theirs. Trouble is, I can't be honest with my readers until I'm honest with one person—the guy I fell in love with.

I need to turn down his job offer. But even if Milo's not ready for romance again, I still want him to know he did more than please my body. He won my heart.

I head inside, scoop up my pup, and park myself at the kitchen table with my best buddy sitting in my lap. I scratch his chin. "You're my man," I tell StudMuffin, even as I long for what could have been.

I flip open my laptop and start a new document.

I have a new top-five list. It's all about how to fulfill your romantic fantasies, and it starts with this simple plan.

Find the person who will encourage your dreams. The one who'll believe in you, even when you don't believe in yourself.

That's a good start. I stare at the ceiling, noodling on the next bit when I hear a thud.

Then a loud *psst.*

Then the buzzing of my phone.

I squeak when Milo's name flashes on my screen. I open the text instantly.

Milo: Look on your balcony, sunshine.

Gasping, I jump up from the table, rush to the deck, and find the paper airplane in the corner. But paper airplanes don't fly solo. They need captains.

I peer over the balcony, and I can't stop the grin from spreading when I spot the pilot. There he is, waving and looking hopeful as he holds a . . . panini?

"Did you open the airplane?" Milo calls up.

"Not yet," I say, then bend to grab it. As I stand, I unfold it with excited fingers, then read his note.

I don't want to call it good. I want to call you my girlfriend. But I'd be a terrible boyfriend if I left your fantasy unfulfilled. I believe you wanted a panini. Shame on me for never making you one. I did tonight, and I have so much to tell you, if you'll have me, my Naughty, Amazing, Wonderful Juliet.

My heart does the rhumba as I gaze down at the man professing his love from the street. "I will definitely have you and the sandwich," I shout as joy fills my entire body.

He smiles and it suits him so well, that beautiful, happy gaze. "I'm on my way, but first I need to tell you something," he says, cupping his mouth. "I'm falling in love with you, Veronica Valentine."

I laugh, and I smile, and I run to the door to unlock it. A few seconds later, he's up the stairs and scooping me into his arms.

When he kisses me, my toes curl, and my heart sings.

Milo breaks the kiss, then says, "Correction: I am in love with you."

"I'm in love with you too," I say, then I tug him into my home, and shut the door.

I'm pretty sure I'm going to have more than sex and sandwiches. It'll be sex and sandwiches and love.

But first, I want the balcony fantasy to come true in every single way.

32

A DOG'S LIFE

Milo

The problem with balcony fantasies is this—people walk by on the street below.

Exhibitionism is totally cool, but it's not my thing, nor is it Veronica's.

But if there are life hacks for making wine ice cubes, then there are life hacks for balcony banging.

It's called—wait for it—a chair. I snag one from the kitchen table, haul it to the balcony, and pull her into my lap. That'll obscure us from the street. I unzip my shorts while she yanks off her panties. After I slide on a condom, she sinks onto me.

I sizzle. She feels so good.

Then, I feel electric when she gasps and leans her head back.

"Yes, I knew it," she whispers. "I already love balcony sex with Mister Sexy Pants."

"You are easy to please." I laugh, then lean in to kiss the hollow of her throat. Her orange blossom scent makes me dizzy, and the heat of her makes me high.

She ropes her arms around my neck, finding a rhythm as she rides me.

I can't believe I nearly lost her. Threading my fingers through her hair, I tug her face close to mine. "Don't want to give you up," I tell her.

"Then don't," she counters as she rises up then sinks back down. My legs shake with lust. My head swims with happiness.

We rock and thrust under the fading sun as New York rolls on by beyond the balcony.

Here, above the city, we come back together.

* * *

After, she eats the grilled cheese and avocado panini I made for her, moaning in a foodgasm at the kitchen table. "Tell me about the ride," she says in between bites.

"It was great aside from the part where I was completely miserable and ornery, thinking I lost you. I spent the first day in the saddle contemplating what a dumbass I was to let you go and what a 'fraidy cat I was to allow my ex to control my dating life," I say.

"Aww, that's so sweet," she teases, then dabs at the corner of her mouth with a gingham napkin.

"Yes, it was sweet being an ogre. My friends knocked some sense into me, and I realized I needed to start a list of my own."

Her eyebrows rise in intrigue. "Keep going. I love lists."

I tap my temple. "I keep it up here, but it's basically a list of things you like and how I can give them to you in and out of bed," I say, gesturing to the vanishing sandwich. "Like that. That's the first thing."

"I very much approve," she says. "What else is on it?"

I park my chin in my hand. "Take you out on a proper date tomorrow night. And this weekend too. Maybe even get you cake."

"Mmm. I do like cake," she says, then takes another bite of the sandwich.

"Buying you . . . *gifties*," I say, in my dirtiest tone.

"Yep. You're a keeper," she says, finishing her sandwich, then wiping her hands. "But I'm working on a list too."

I curl my fingers, beckoning for her to share. She grabs her laptop from the edge of the table, flips it open, then clicks on her mouse. She gives me a soft, almost shy look. "I started it right before you showed up at my balcony. I didn't get far, but it's a top-five list of what makes a great partner," she says, then shows me a file.

She's only written a few lines, but they restore my faith in romance. As I read her words, *Find the person who will encourage your dreams. The one who'll believe in you, even when you don't believe in yourself,* I don't think dating leads to disasters anymore.

It led me to her.

"C'mere," I whisper.

She stands, moves around the table, and joins me,

sitting on my lap once again. I nuzzle her neck. "I'm so glad you tossed glitter on me," I murmur.

She laughs. "I did not toss it on you. The glitter threw up on your beard."

I rub my whiskers against her jawline. "Whatever you say."

She swats my shoulder. "And to think I was going to tell you the rest of my list."

I lift my face and adopt a sweet smile. "Tell me."

Her vulnerable eyes meet mine. "I wrote this in my head the other morning. It's what I wanted to say to you then. *Find the person who fixes your broken cabinet, kisses your tears, and lifts your spirits. Also, ideally, the one who fucks you just the way you want.*"

Yup. My radar *is* working again. Everything beeps for her. I kiss her deeply, feeling calm and settled. She's where I'm meant to be.

But I also have a dog to walk. When we separate, I suggest we meet on the street with the four-legged beasts.

After I grab my pup from my home and meet her outside, we walk through the neighborhood under a starry sky. "So, what did you do while I was off banging my head against the brick wall of my . . . head?"

She laughs, then nudges me. "Started a business."

"Oh, just that?" I tease, then realize there was a touch of pride in her tone. When I read her face—vulnerable and serious—I drop the teasing. "Wow. I can't wait to hear everything."

"It's called Date Night for One . . ."

* * *

Twenty minutes later I'm toasting with champagne at the bar where we had our first date. "Congratulations. It's so you, Veronica. It's perfect," I say.

She clinks back. "Thank you. And I'll stick around Bikes and Blooms until you find another manager. I'll miss it. I truly enjoyed working with you, but I think this new business is my heart."

"I think so too. And I followed mine with the shop. You should follow yours. I'll find someone to replace you," I say earnestly.

No one can replace her, but I don't say that. She should be free to pursue her dreams with no worries.

Her business is a genius idea.

Just like she had brilliant suggestions at the shop.

Which makes me think . . .

"What if you offered the subscription box at the store too? Let's be honest. Sex and flowers do go together."

Her eyes sparkle. "I would love that. And when you start, it can be National Battery Day."

I laugh, then toast to her once more. When we're done, I take her home, and we cross off another item on her list as we get under the covers.

Well, she didn't include two dogs watching us sixty-nine, but a dog's gotta do what a dog's gotta do.

33

THE VIRGIN CLUB ALUMNI

Veronica

Things We Assume About the Deflowered

I've heard them all.

Just get it over with.

Find someone to bang and move on.

Who cares who he is? He'll never stick around anyway.

But I've never followed conventional wisdom. Do what works for you, I say.

I waited twenty-six years to have intercourse. I don't regret taking my time. Here's why.

First, I excel at having sex with myself.

Second, the guy was worth waiting for. And I know because I didn't just fall into bed with him. We fell into love. Big, wild, messy, happy, glittery love.

Remember the guy I almost smashed into on the street? The one I flashed my panties to?

He's mine now.

And sometimes reality exceeds expectations. Like when Mister Sexy Pants became Mister Right.

EPILOGUE
BIG PAWS, MY ASS

Hot Stuff

Ahem.

Time to set the record straight. It had come to Hot Stuff's attention that there were some, should we say, misrepresentations of him?

He'd put up with these erroneous perceptions for long enough. He'd allowed certain parties to believe he was simply, well, like a dog.

Dogs didn't plan things. Dogs didn't devise strategies.

But cats? They were thinkers. All that time sleeping was simply a ruse. Cats used those supposedly dreamy hours to plot all sorts of deeds.

And seriously? At this point, couldn't everyone see what had truly gone down?

Fine, fine. He would have to spell it out. He had excellent ears, and a sharp mind after all. And he'd heard *everything*. Every single, solitary detail about Mister Sexy Pants.

Every time his human had swept out to the balcony, that device in her hand—her big hand, he might add—he'd listened. He'd heard. And of course, he'd understood.

The woman wanted the man and blah, blah, blah.

But while he wished he was nefarious enough to send emails, alas, he was not. His plotting was more of the what plant to knock over variety. What keyboard to sit on. What mug to bat to the ground.

It was fun when things broke.

He couldn't help it. He was drawn to machines and to the chance to destroy them. Such was a cat's life.

In any case, he digressed.

Occupational hazard of being a cat.

The point was this—*big paws, my ass*.

His paws were fucking fabulous.

EPILOGUE
HEAD-TO-HEAD COMPETITION

Veronica

A Year Later

Milo rushes to the door, finger-combing his hair. He's going to be so late for work. But that's the risk with morning sex, and I have no regrets.

Sometimes you get carried away when you wake up next to an inked, bearded babe who loves you madly.

I help him along by hooking Trudy to a leash and handing him the strap.

He flashes a dirty grin as he takes the leash. "Is it obvious I just got some?"

I raise a brow. "You want it to be obvious for all your employees?"

"Hmm. Good point. I should be professional," he

says, intensely serious. "Especially since it's National Solo Flight Day."

The chalkboard outside his shop will greet customers with the words: *Love Yourself a Lily More Today.*

"And Felix already texted me and said the online orders are ticking up for lilies," I say. Felix is the new flower shop manager. My mom recommended him. He trained at her garden shop in Connecticut and wanted to move into the city, so the florist job was a perfect fit. Plus, Mom enjoyed matchmaking—she loves Felix, and she loves Milo, and she wanted to help.

How could she *not* love my boyfriend? He won her heart when I introduced them nearly a year ago at a dinner in the city at my favorite sandwich shop. He won Hazel's heart too. And Ellie's. That's his style. He's outgoing and clever, and he likes people.

Good thing I do too.

I also enjoy people-watching, especially when it involves my sister and a certain friend of Milo's.

One night, when Bryan comes back to town for part of the summer, my boyfriend and I gather the crew at the arcade, then split into teams at the Skee-Ball machines. Drew says he can handle the game solo and it's only fair to the rest of us since no matter what team he was on, he'd win. Probably true with that arm of his. Ellie grabs Bryan for her team, saying she needs to catch up with him. I go with my guy, which leaves my sister scowling at the tall, broody, blue-eyed Axel Huxley, who's even broodier in that leather jacket, leaning against the wall by the last Skee-Ball machine, looking dangerous and smart.

"I can play solo too," Hazel insists, all tough girl.

"It's your special skill," Axel grumbles.

"Are you sure about that? I'd say it's yours, Huxley," Hazel retorts.

The thriller writer unleashes a killer grin. "Your memory might need some work, Valentine."

In slow motion, I turn my wide-eyed gaze to Ellie, silently asking, *Did you hear that?*

She nods big and long. *Yes, I did,* she mouths.

"You have a lot of senses that need a tune-up," Hazel says. "Shall I list them?"

Fear flashes in Axel's eyes, but then he shrugs it off. "Maybe save it for the next book, sweetheart."

She doubles down by crossing her arms. "Aww, it still hurts, doesn't it?"

"Ouch, does someone need some aloe?" Milo cuts in, then gently slides me in the direction of my sister. "Valentine ladies can play together. I'll take my *lawyer.*"

Milo teams up with his friend, but all through the game, I catch Axel staring at my sister, and I don't think that's anger in his eyes.

More like red-hot lust.

When we finish the round—with Drew winning and the Valentines coming in second—my sister marches over to Axel.

* * *

Hazel

· · ·

This man. I have never known a creature, real or fictional, to inflame me so much. I tap Axel on the shoulder. "We need to talk."

He arches a cocky brow because of course his eyebrows are cocky. Every single body part is, I bet.

"Sweetheart, I'm not sure you *can* talk," he drawls. "You just want to argue."

"Like you don't," I hiss.

"I can be civil. Want me to show you?"

"I can be civil too," I whisper, but I won't if I stay here with him while he winds me up in front of everyone. That's what he does. Pushes all my buttons.

Grabbing his arm — his too-strong, too muscular arm, damn him — I march him into the game room. I stop at an ACDC pinball machine, then wheel around and meet his eyes. He returns my stare with a smirk. A fucking smirk.

Why is he like this? Can't he just get over what happened? I take a deep breath, try to let it settle me. "Look, Huxley. I don't like this any more than you do."

"Like what?" He asks, feigning innocence.

I sigh, aggrieved. Then point from him to me, then out to *them*. "The fact that you and I have to hang out because my sister's in love with your friend, who, by the way is an amazing guy."

"He is. Milo's good people," Axel says warmly.

That's why I have to try to bury the hatchet. But it's big and it's thick. "If it were up to me, we'd never see each other again, but clearly we have to. So, we need to find a way to get along," I say diplomatically.

His lips twitch. "You really want that?"

No. But I don't want my latent irritation over every single thing that went wrong when we tried to work together to send me over the edge. "Yes. Can we just please put the past behind us?"

He hums, like he's considering it. "So, you truly want to get along, Valentine?"

I burn inside. When his bedroom eyes roam up and down my body, I burn hot.

Hotter still when he steps closer to me.

"I do want to," I say, breath catching dangerously, pulse surging.

"Then I have some good ideas," he says, and the way I react to his smoky voice is entirely unfair.

Must. Resist. At. All. Costs.

Veronica

With Hazel off in the game room, I spin around and head straight for Ellie and Bryan at the bar.

"So, that's what he said," Bryan remarks as I near them.

Ellie slugs his shoulder playfully. "And then? What did you say?" She's on the edge of her seat.

Bryan takes his time answering, giving a half smile, maybe a little resigned. "Well, it's complicated."

They stop talking when I arrive. I tilt my head, like *c'mon*. "It was just getting good. Are you freezing me out?"

Bryan laughs, then shakes his head. "No. It's just that it's *really* complicated."

I grab a stool and park my chin in my hand. "I'm listening."

"So, Sebastian Lowe hired my company . . ."

As Bryan unravels more of the story, my breath hitches.

"Complicated barely scratches the surface," I say, a little amazed and pretty damn intrigued to hear how their story plays out.

"Maybe you could write the rest of it, Ellie," Bryan offers.

Ellie's ventured down the scriptwriting path after all, trying her hand at writing TV shows. *Future-proofing against the inevitable*, she says. At Bryan's suggestion, her eyes spark. "Not a bad idea. Thanks so much for giving me the rights in advance to your sexy tale," she says, adding a wink.

"Did I say it was sexy?" Bryan smiles.

Ellie laughs. "No. I figured that part out on my own."

Milo's brother just smiles, then turns the tables on her. "And what about you and your guy?"

Ellie sighs, a little wistful. As she updates him, I listen, grateful my love life isn't complicated anymore.

It's simply wonderful.

* * *

One morning, a little later that summer, I settle in at the table. I work from home, with my dog and my cat, and I don't usually wear any pants.

This is the life—writing my column and putting together orders for Date Night for One, curating a delicious box of treats for the ladies who want a little help from a battery-operated friend.

Business is thriving, and I don't miss publishing. Pleasure is where my heart lies.

But it also lies with my man and our dogs.

When I finish working in the evening, I put on a sundress, say goodbye to the cat, and leash up StudMuffin. After I head down the stairs, I grab my custom bike from the storage closet in our building—Milo moved in with me months ago.

Then I wheel my ride to the sidewalk and set my dog in the tiny bike seat Milo built for him. StudMuffin used to hate bikes, but living with a bike lover has turned him around. Well, my little man doesn't love bikes per se. But he sure does love riding in the front and checking out the city as we go. When my blond babe is buckled in, I strap on his little helmet, then kiss his wet nose.

After I clip on my own helmet, I zip across town to meet my boyfriend for a picnic in Gramercy Square Park.

It's a gated park, but Milo has a friend with a key, so he waits for me outside, on his bike, with his pooch in her seat. We lock up the bikes, then bring our dogs into the park.

We grab a bench and dive into the picnic dinner Milo brought along as the pups sit at our feet.

"So I had this one customer today who asked for a recommendation for *something extra strong*, and then said, *And Veronica will know what I mean*," Milo tells me. "You're basically famous there. It's Bikes, Blooms, and Buzz."

"And I'm sure I have just the thing for her," I say with a smile. "You'll give me her info?"

"I always do," he says, then he snaps his fingers. "Oh, and there's one more thing I forgot to tell you."

I meet his gaze again, curious. "What is it?"

"Actually, it's something I wanted to ask you," he corrects, then slides off the bench, and in one fluid move, he's dropped down to one knee.

I gasp, my hand flying to my mouth as he reaches for my other hand.

"Veronica Valentine, I thought the day you walked into that cake shop was the best day of my life. Then, the day your dog attacked my bike was an even better day. And then the next day became the best when we talked on the street. And every single day we spend together is better than the last," he says, and my heart thumps wildly in my chest. He reaches into his pocket and pulls out a blue velvet box. "I'm so glad we kept crashing into each other's world and so thrilled our timing was a hot mess, because when we finally came together, I *knew*. You were the one for me. I want to keep having the best days with you because you're the greatest part of my life. And I love you madly."

As he takes a beat, a tear slides down one of my cheeks, then the other.

He leans in, kisses them gently away, then meets my gaze once more. "Will you be Mrs. Sexy Pants?"

And I smile and cry as I throw my arms around him. "That's the most perfect proposal ever," I say, then he slides a sapphire solitaire on my finger.

I gaze at it in joyful wonder. I love that it's unique, like him, and like us.

I truly have the best guy in the world.

I kiss him once more as my dog licks my hand and his dog kisses his cheek.

Fine, *we* have the best dogs too.

Want more from this crew? Keep flipping for a sexy short story! And check out Hazel's and Axel's romance FREE in KU in **My So-Called Sex Life**!

Binge read all The Dating Games standalones for FREE IN KU!

Two A Day: Drew and Brooke:
The Good Guy Challenge: Ellie and Gabe
My So-Called Sex Life: Hazel and Axel

And keep reading for an excerpt from Hazel's romance!

EXCERPT - MY SO-CALLED SEX LIFE

Chapter One

Hazel

Obviously, I believe in love.

If I didn't, I'd be the worst kind of romance writer—the kind who lies to her readers.

But there's something I believe in more fervently than love, and that's the meet-cute. You can't get to the happy ending without the unputdownable beginning.

The start of the story is my writing church, and I worship at the altar of those delicious moments when the hero and heroine meet for the first time.

Or meet again.

Tonight, I'll be researching a new here's-how-they-met possibility as I head to dinner in New York.

I'm one block away from the restaurant. My short,

black ankle boots click against the sidewalk on Twenty-Fourth Street as I gaze up at the numbers on the buildings. I pass a tattoo parlor where a goth gal inks a burly man's arm, and then I acquire the target.

Menu.

"It's as trendy as it is annoying," my friend TJ said of the joint when he told me about it last week. "And I promise it'll inspire your next chapter one."

I was sold. I made a reservation right away.

Now, I'm here at the minimalist-style restaurant. Under the sign for Menu are the words *Meet, Eat, Mingle.*

Change your life.

Ambitious, but the way I see it, this place is going to be full of fodder. I can't wait. I draw a deep inhale of the May night air, then square my shoulders. "Cover me, I'm going in," I say to, well, no one.

Sometimes I talk to myself. It's a thing. Whatever.

I head inside, marching to the hostess stand. A woman wearing a black tunic and sporting a blonde undercut shoots me a bored look. Yeah, that's on point for a place called Menu.

"Hello. I have a reservation. Valentine. Party of one," I say.

"It's all parties of one," she says, monotone.

"Old habit," I say with a friendly shrug. "In any case, it's for seven-thirty."

With an aggrieved sigh, she scans the tablet screen, then meets my eyes. "The other party isn't here yet. If he or she is five minutes late, we'll have to ask you to leave."

Okaaaay.

It's a new world order. Restaurants have rigid rules. But I knew what I'd signed up for. "Works for me," I say. You catch more flies with honey and all.

"Fine," she says, then she nods toward the dining room behind her. It's small and bare, in keeping with the theme, aka *we're cool, you're not.* The tables are black wood, the walls are steel gray, the tiles are white. Everything is ordinary, except the experience.

This restaurant is très chic because it seats strangers together.

As I follow her, I smile, giddy at the thought of an inspired meet-cute. Two sexy strangers happen to be seated together at a hipster restaurant just like this. They hit it off. Get it on that night. Then, oops! The next day he turns out to be her brand-new boss, perhaps?

But who is he? A mafia king? A sexy CEO?

The muses will let me know who the next hero is. Maybe he'll even reveal himself tonight.

Undercut brings me to a table at the back. She waves a limp hand in the direction of the framed QR code on the black wood surface. "We use QR codes. You scan them with your phone. Have you ever used one before?"

I'm thirty-one, missy. I can work a phone, a power drill, and a twenty-speed vibrator. Not all at once though. "I'm familiar with the concept of QR codes. Also, phones," I say.

"Cool," she says blandly, then walks away, her tunic swishing against her leggings.

Once I sit, I rub my palms on my jeans, a tiny bit

nervous. What if I'm seated with an over-sharer? An endless talker? A dullsville candidate?

But I'm excited too.

What if my companion is an enigmatic billionaire like in a romance novel? A broody rock musician? A hot tech nerd who's looking for a matchmaker?

Gah. The meet-cute possibilities are endless, and when I write this as the opening of my next book, it's going to be epic.

I just know it.

I'm making some notes on my phone about the vibe when a man's voice interrupts my thoughts.

"Four minutes and forty-five seconds." His tone is a little gravelly and a lot know-it-all-y.

Say it isn't so.

I was already dreading sharing a stage with Axel Huxley at the reader expo I'm doing this weekend. I can't believe fate would inflict him on me any sooner than necessary.

I turn my gaze toward the front of Menu, praying that's not my archnemesis. Maybe he has a vocal twin. Maybe that's a thing now.

But my prayers are unanswered. Standing tall at the hostess stand is the smart-mouthed, glasses-wearing, smirky-faced romantic-thriller writer.

Wearing black because of course he wears black.

And *of course* he's arguing with the hostess. He never met a statement he couldn't debate and dissect into a million julienned pieces, then pepper with disagreement.

He blah blah blahs a little more, finishing with, "So, you have to seat me. It's the policy of the restaurant."

I snort. *Get over yourself, Huxley. I hope they kick you out.*

I feel sorry for whichever sucker is getting seated with King Dick tonight.

Inspired, I make another note, chuckling fiendishly as I imagine my heroine running into her enemy before the clever, charming, hottie hero enters the scene. Then I check the menu options while waiting for my brilliant professor, my inscrutable tycoon, my good guy with a heart of gold in need of a makeover.

Until the sound of footsteps grows louder and closer. I look up.

At a face I want to punch.

Keep reading: My So-Called Sex-Life!

BE A LOVELY

Want to be the first to know of sales, new releases, special deals and giveaways? Sign up for my newsletter today!

Want to be part of a fun, feel-good place to talk about books and romance, and get sneak peeks of covers and advance copies of my books? Be a Lovely!

MORE BOOKS BY LAUREN

I've written more than 100 books! **All of these titles below are FREE in Kindle Unlimited!**

Double Pucked

A sexy, outrageous MFM hockey romantic comedy!

Puck Yes

A fake marriage, spicy MFM hockey rom com!

Thoroughly Pucked!

A brother's best friends +runaway bride, spicy MFM hockey rom com!

The Virgin Society Series

Meet the Virgin Society – great friends who'd do anything for each other. Indulge in these forbidden, emotionally-charged, and wildly sexy age-gap romances!

The RSVP

The Tryst

The Tease

The Dating Games Series

A fun, sexy romantic comedy series about friends in the city and their dating mishaps!

The Virgin Next Door

Two A Day

The Good Guy Challenge

How To Date Series (New and ongoing)

Friends who are like family. Chances to learn how to date again. Standalone romantic comedies full of love, sex and meet-cute shenanigans.

My So-Called Sex Life

Plays Well With Others

The Almost Romantic

Juliet's And Monroe's Romance (coming in June 2024)

Sawyer's Romance with Mystery Woman (August 2024)

Wilder's and Fable's Romance (November 2024)

Boyfriend Material

Four fabulous heroines. Four outrageous proposals. Four chances at love in this sexy rom-com series!

Asking For a Friend

Sex and Other Shiny Objects

One Night Stand-In

Overnight Service

Big Rock Series

My #1 New York Times Bestselling sexy as sin, irreverent, male-POV romantic comedy!

Big Rock

Mister O

Well Hung

Full Package

Joy Ride

Hard Wood

Friends in New York City and California fall in love in this fun and hot rom-com series!

Birthday Suit

Dear Sexy Ex-Boyfriend

The What If Guy

Thanks for Last Night

The Dream Guy Next Door

Always Satisfied Series

A group of friends in New York City find love and laughter in this series of sexy standalones!

Satisfaction Guaranteed

Never Have I Ever

Instant Gratification

PS It's Always Been You

The Gift Series

An after dark series of standalones! Explore your fantasies!

The Engagement Gift

The Virgin Gift

The Decadent Gift

The Heartbreakers Series

Three brothers. Three rockers. Three standalone sexy romantic comedies.

Once Upon a Real Good Time

Once Upon a Sure Thing

Once Upon a Wild Fling

Sinful Men

A high-stakes, high-octane, sexy-as-sin romantic suspense series!

My Sinful Nights

My Sinful Desire

My Sinful Longing

My Sinful Love

My Sinful Temptation

From Paris With Love

Swoony, sweeping romances set in Paris!

Wanderlust

Part-Time Lover

One Love Series

A group of friends in New York falls in love one by one in this sexy rom-com series!

The Sexy One

The Hot One

The Knocked Up Plan

Come As You Are

Lucky In Love Series

A small town romance full of heat and blue collar heroes and sexy heroines!

Best Laid Plans

The Feel Good Factor

Nobody Does It Better

Unzipped

No Regrets

An angsty, sexy, emotional, new adult trilogy about one young couple fighting to break free of their pasts!

The Start of Us

The Thrill of It

Every Second With You

The Caught Up in Love Series

A group of friends finds love!

The Pretending Plot

The Dating Proposal

The Second Chance Plan

The Private Rehearsal

Seductive Nights Series

A high heat series full of danger and spice!

Night After Night

After This Night

One More Night

A Wildly Seductive Night

Joy Delivered Duet

A high-heat, wickedly sexy series of standalones that will set your sheets on fire!

Nights With Him

Forbidden Nights

Unbreak My Heart

A standalone second chance emotional roller coaster of a romance

The Muse

A magical realism romance set in Paris

Good Love Series of sexy rom-coms co-written with Lili Valente!

I also write MM romance under the name L. Blakely!

Hopelessly Bromantic Duet (MM)

Roomies to lovers to enemies to fake boyfriends

Hopelessly Bromantic

Here Comes My Man

Men of Summer Series (MM)

Two baseball players on the same team fall in love in a forbidden romance spanning five epic years

Scoring With Him

Winning With Him

All In With Him

MM Standalone Novels

A Guy Walks Into My Bar

The Bromance Zone

One Time Only

The Best Men (Co-written with Sarina Bowen)

Winner Takes All Series (MM)

A series of emotionally-charged and irresistibly sexy standalone MM sports romances!

The Boyfriend Comeback

Turn Me On

A Very Filthy Game

Limited Edition Husband

Manhandled

If you want a personalized recommendation, email me at laurenblakelybooks@gmail.com!

CONTACT

You can find Lauren on Instagram at LaurenBlakelyBooks, Facebook at LaurenBlakelyBooks, or online at LaurenBlakely.com. You can also email her at laurenblakelybooks@gmail.com